The Tempest

BESTSELLING FICTION

- 1984 by George Orwell
  Fiction/Classics, ISBN: 9788193545836
- Animal Farm by George Orwell
  Fiction/Classics, ISBN: 9789387669062
- Anthem by Ayn Rand
  Fiction/Classics, ISBN: 9789389157178
- As a Man Thinketh by James Allen
  Fiction/Classics, ISBN: 9789388118422
- Demian by Hermann Hesse
  Fiction/Classics, ISBN: 9789388118170
- Gitanjali by Rabindranath Tagore
  Fiction/Poems, ISBN: 9789387669079
- Mansarover 1 (Hindi) by Premchand
  Fiction/Short Stories, ISBN: 9789387669086
- Selected Stories of Rabindranath Tagore by Tagore
  Fiction/Short Stories, ISBN: 9789387669307
- Siddhartha by Hermann Hesse
  Fiction/Classics, ISBN: 9789387669116
- Tales from India by Rudyard Kipling
  Fiction/Short Stories, ISBN: 9789387669123
- Tales from Shakespeare by Charles Lamb, Mary Lamb
  Fiction/Short Stories, ISBN: 9789387669314
- The Jungle Book by Rudyard Kipling
  Children's/Classics, ISBN: 9789387669338
- The Light of Asia by Sir Edwin Arnold
  Fiction/Poetry, ISBN: 9789387669130
- The Prophet by Kahlil Gibran
  Fiction/Classics, ISBN: 9789388118453

Search the book by its ISBN

The Tempest

William Shakespeare

GENERAL PRESS

Published by

GENERAL PRESS

4805/24, Fourth Floor, Krishna House
Ansari Road, Daryaganj, New Delhi - 110002
Ph : 011-23282971, 45795759
E-mail : generalpressindia@gmail.com

www.generalpress.in

First Edition : 2022

ISBN : 9789354993701

Published by Azeem Ahmad Khan for General Press

Contents

William Shakespeare

William Shakespeare (1564–1616), an English playwright and poet was born and brought up in Stratford-upon-Avon. He is generally considered the greatest dramatist the world has ever known and the finest poet who has written in the English language. Shakespeare has also been the world's most popular author. Shakespeare wrote at least 37 plays, which have traditionally been divided into comedies, histories, and tragedies. No other writer's plays have been produced so many times or read so widely in so many countries. These plays contain vivid characters of all types and from many walks of life. Kings, pickpockets, drunkards, generals, hired killers, shepherds, and philosophers, all mingle in Shakespeare's works. His plays are filled with action, his characters are believable, and his language is thrilling to hear or read. His comedies are full of fun. The characters are lively; the dialogues are witty. In the end young lovers are wed; old babblers are silenced; wise men are content. The comedies are joyous and romantic.

Shakespeare was born in a middle-class family. His birthplace was the small market town of Stratford-upon-Avon. Shortly after he married at the age of 18, Shakespeare apparently left Stratford to seek his fortune in the theatrical world of London. Within a few years, he had become one of the city's leading actors and playwrights. By 1612, when he seems to have partially retired to Stratford, Shakespeare had become England's most popular playwright.

William's father – John Shakespeare, was a glove maker who owned a shop in the town of Stratford-upon-Avon. Stratford lies about 75 miles (120 kilometres) northwest of London in the county of Warwickshire. John Shakespeare was a respected man in the town and held several important positions in the local government. William Shakespeare's mother was Mary Arden. She was the daughter of a farmer but related to a family of considerable social standing in the county. John Shakespeare married Mary Arden about 1557. William Shakespeare was born in Stratford in 1564, the third of eight children. The register of Holy Trinity, the parish church in Stratford, records his baptism on April 26. According to the custom at that time, infants were baptized about three days after their birth. Therefore, the generally accepted date for Shakespeare's birth is April 23.

The Shakespeares were a family of considerable local prominence. In 1565, John Shakespeare became an alderman. Three years later, he was elected bailiff (mayor), the highest civic honour that a Stratford resident could receive. Later, he held several other civic posts. But toward the end of his life, John Shakespeare had financial problems.

Beginning at about the age of 7, young William Shakespeare probably attended the Stratford grammar school with other boys of his social class. The school's highly qualified teachers were graduates of Oxford University. Students spent about nine hours a day in school. They attended classes the year around, except for three brief holiday periods. The teachers enforced strict discipline and physically punished students who broke the rules. The students chiefly studied Latin, the language of ancient Rome. Knowledge of Latin was necessary for a career in medicine, law, or the church. In addition, Latin was considered a sign of an educated person.

Young Shakespeare may have read such outstanding ancient Roman authors as Cicero, Ovid, Plautus, Seneca, Terence, and Virgil. In spite of the long hours he spent in school, Shakespeare's boyhood was probably not all boring study. As a market centre, Stratford was a lively town. In addition, holidays provided popular pageants and shows, including plays about the legendary outlaw Robin Hood and his merry men. By 1569, travelling companies of professional actors were performing in Stratford. Stratford also held two large fairs each year, which attracted numerous visitors from other counties. For young Shakespeare, Stratford could thus have been an exciting place to live in.

Stratford also offered Shakespeare other pleasures. The fields and woods surrounding the town provided opportunities to hunt and trap small game. The River Avon, which ran through the town, had fish to catch. Shakespeare's poems and plays show a love of nature and rural life. This display undoubtedly reflects his childhood experiences and his love of the Stratford countryside.

In November 1582, Shakespeare received the licence to marry Anne Hathaway. She was probably the daughter of a farmer who lived in Shottery, a village about one mile (1.6 kilometres) from Stratford. At the time of their marriage, Shakespeare was 18-years old and Anne was 26. Their first child, Susanna, was baptized on May 26, 1583. Early in 1585, Anne Shakespeare gave birth to twins – a boy, Hamnet, and a girl, Judith. No significant factual information exists on Shakespeare's life for the period between February 2, 1585, when the twins were baptized, and 1592, when evidence indicates Shakespeare was living in London. Scholars sometimes call this period the lost years.

There is some indication that Shakespeare had become well known in London's theatrical life by 1592. Sometime after he arrived in London, he probably joined one of the city's repertory theatre companies. These companies consisted of a permanent cast of actors who presented a variety of plays week after week. The companies were commercial organizations that depended on admission prices for their income. They staged most of the plays Londoners attended. By 1594, at least six of Shakespeare's plays had been produced.

From mid-1592 to 1594, London authorities often closed the public theatres because of repeated outbreaks of plague. The need for new plays thus declined. At this time, Shakespeare began to write poems. The Elizabethans considered the writing of poetry much more important than the writing of plays. Shakespeare perhaps believed that by writing poems he might be able to win the praise that mere playwriting never received. In 1593, Shakespeare's long poem *Venus and Adonis* was printed by Richard Field, a Stratford neighbour who had become a London printer. *Venus and Adonis* quickly became a success. Field printed Shakespeare's next long poem, *The Rape of Lucrece*, in 1594. Both poems went through many editions during Shakespeare's lifetime, but their success did not lead Shakespeare to give up playwriting. After the public theatres were reopened in 1594, he began again to write plays.

From 1594 to 1608, Shakespeare was fully involved in the London theatre world. In addition to his duties as a stockholder and actor in the Lord Chamberlain's Men, he wrote an average of almost two plays a year for his company. During much of this period, Shakespeare ranked as London's most popular playwright, based on the number of times his plays were performed and published. But his reputation was largely that of a popular playwright, not of a writer of unequalled genius. Few people gave him the praise that later generations heaped on him. An exception was the English clergyman and schoolmaster Francis Meres. In 1598, Meres wrote *Palladis Tamia: Wit's Treasury*, a book that has become an important source of information about Shakespeare's career.

In this book, Meres said of Shakespeare: "As *Plautus* and *Seneca* are accounted the best for comedy and tragedy among the Latins: so Shakespeare among the English is the most excellent in both kinds for the stage." Although Meres' praise did not represent everyone's opinion, it indicates that Shakespeare had become an established writer by at least the late 1590's. And he had not yet written most of his great tragedies, such as *Hamlet, Othello, King Lear*, and *Macbeth*.

By the late 1590's, Shakespeare had not only become an established writer, but he had also become prosperous. In 1597, he purchased New Place, one of the two largest houses in Stratford. Shakespeare obviously remained a Stratford man at heart in spite of his busy, successful life in London. Records of business dealings and of minor lawsuits reveal that he preferred to invest most of his money in Stratford rather than in London. In 1599, Shakespeare and six associates became owners of the Globe, a new outdoor theatre in the London suburb of Southwark. The Globe was one of the largest theatres in the London area. It may have held as many as 3,000 spectators.

From 1599 to 1608 was a period of extraordinary literary activity for Shakespeare. During these years, he wrote several comedies and almost all the tragedies that have made him famous. Shakespeare's masterpieces during this period include the comedies – *Much Ado About Nothing* and *Twelfth Night*; the history – *Henry V*; and the tragedies – *Antony and Cleopatra, Hamlet, Julius Caesar, King Lear, Macbeth,* and *Othello*. During his last eight years of life, Shakespeare wrote only four plays – *Cymbeline, Henry VIII, The Tempest*, and *The Winter's Tale*. In the past, some scholars argued that *The Tempest*, written about 1610, was Shakespeare's last play. They stated that he then retired almost completely to Stratford. However, *Henry VIII* can be dated about 1613. In addition, Shakespeare purchased a house in the Blackfriars district of London in 1613. The evidence thus suggests that Shakespeare gradually reduced his activity in London rather than ending it abruptly.

Shakespeare's influence on language has not been limited to writers and scholars. Many words and phrases from Shakespeare's plays and poems have become part of our everyday speech. They are used by millions of people who are unaware that Shakespeare created them. For example, Shakespeare originated such familiar phrases as fair play, a foregone conclusion, catch cold, and disgraceful conduct. As far as scholars can tell, Shakespeare also invented such common words as assassination, bump, eventful, and lonely.

Shakespeare must have divided his time between his private life in Stratford and his public life in London. He had lodgings in London at least until 1604 and probably until 1611. Yet such family events as his daughter Susanna's marriage in 1607 and his mother's death in 1608 would certainly have called him back to Stratford. By 1612, he may have been spending much of his time in the comforts of New Place in Stratford.

On February 10, 1616, Shakespeare's younger daughter, Judith, married Thomas Quiney, the son of his Stratford neighbour Richard Quiney. Six weeks later, Shakespeare revised his will. Within a month, he died. He was buried inside the Stratford parish church. His monument records the day of death as April 23, the generally accepted date of his birth. Shakespeare's son, Hamnet, died in 1596 at the age of 11. The playwright's daughter Susanna had one child, Elizabeth, who bore no children. Judith gave birth to three boys, but they died before she did. Shakespeare's last direct descendant, his granddaughter, Elizabeth, died in 1670.

For readers interested in a specific play or plays, the following table lists the plays alphabetically:

All's Well That Ends Well

Antony and Cleopatra

As You Like It

Comedy of Errors, The

Coriolanus

Cymbeline

Hamlet

Henry IV, Parts I and II

Henry V

Henry VI, Parts I, II, and III

Henry VII

Julius Caesar

King John

King Lear

Love's Labour's Lost

Macbeth

Measure for Measure

Merchant of Venice, The

Merry Wives of Windsor, The

Midsummer's Night Dream, A

Much Ado About Nothing

Othello

Pericles

Richard II

Richard III

Romeo and Juliet

Taming of the Shrew, The

Tempest, The

Timon of Athens

Titus Andronicus

Troilus and Cressida

Twelfth Night

Two Gentlemen of Verona, The

Characters in the Play

PROSPERO, *rightful Duke of Millaine (Milan).*

MIRANDA, *Prospero's daughter.*

ARIEL, *a spirit serving Prospero.*

Other serving SPIRITS *appearing as 'shapes', hounds, etc., and as characters (deities, nymphs and shepherds) in a masque.*

CALIBAN, *Prospero's slave.*

ALONSO, *King of Naples.*

SEBASTIAN, *Alonso's brother.*

FERDINAND, *Alonso's son.*

ANTONIO, *Prospero's brother, the usurping Duke of Millaine.*

GONZALO, *an elderly councillor.*

STEPHANO, *Alonso's butler.*

TRINCULO, *Alonso's jester.*

MASTER *of a ship.*

BOATSWAIN.

MARINERS.

ADRIAN *and* FRANCISCO, *Lords.*

ACT 1

Scene 1. *Main deck of ship. A tempestuous noise of thunder and lightning heard.*

Enter SHIP-MASTER *and* BOATSWAIN.

MASTER Boatswain!

BOATSWAIN Here, master: what cheer?

MASTER Good; speak to th' mariners: fall to't – yarely – or we run ourselves aground. Bestir, bestir. [*Exit.*

Enter MARINERS.

BOATSWAIN Heigh my hearts! Cheerly, cheerly my hearts! Yare, yare: take in the topsail; tend to th' master's whistle. [*To the gale:*] Blow till thou burst thy wind, if room enough!

Enter ALONSO, SEBASTIAN, ANTONIO, FERDINAND, GONZALO *and* OTHERS.

ALONSO Good boatswain, have care. Where's the master ? [*To the mariners:*] Play the men.

BOATSWAIN I pray now, keep below.

ANTONIO Where is the master, bosun?

BOATSWAIN Do you not hear him? You mar our labour. Keep your cabins: you do assist the storm.

GONZALO Nay, good, be patient.

BOATSWAIN When the sea is. Hence! What cares these roarers for the name of king? To cabin; silence! Trouble us not.

GONZALO Good, yet remember whom thou hast aboard.

BOATSWAIN None that I more love than myself. You are a councillor: if you can command these elements to silence, and work the peace of the present, we will not hand a rope more: use your authority. If you cannot, give thanks you have lived so long, and make yourself ready in your cabin for the mischance of the hour, if it so hap. – Cheerly, good hearts! Out of our way, I say.

[*Exit.*

GONZALO I have great comfort from this fellow. Methinks he hath no drowning mark upon him: his complexion is perfect gallows. Stand fast, good Fate, to his hanging; make the rope of his destiny our cable, for our own doth little advantage. If he be not born to be hanged, our case is miserable. [*Exeunt.*

Enter BOATSWAIN.

BOATSWAIN Down with the topmast: yare, lower, lower! Bring her to try with main-course. [*A cry is heard within.*] A plague upon this howling! They are louder than the weather or our office.

Enter SEBASTIAN, ANTONIO *and* GONZALO.

Yet again? What do you here? Shall we give o'er and drown? Have you a mind to sink?

SEBASTIAN A pox o' your throat, you bawling, blasphemous, incharitable dog!

BOATSWAIN Work you, then.

ANTONIO Hang, cur; hang, you whoreson, insolent noise-marker!
We are less afraid to be drowned than thou art.

GONZALO I'll warrant him for drowning, though the ship were no stronger than a nutshell, and as leaky as an unstaunched wench.

BOATSWAIN Lay her a-hold, a-hold! Set her two courses: off to sea again! Lay her off!

Enter MARINERS, *wet.*

MARINERS All lost! To prayers, to prayers! All lost!

BOATSWAIN What, must our mouths be cold?

GONZALO The King and Prince at prayers, let's assist them,
For our case is as theirs.

SEBASTIAN I'm out of patience.

ANTONIO We are merely cheated of our lives by drunkards.
This wide-chapped rascal – would thou mightst lie drowning
The washing of ten tides!

GONZALO He'll be hanged yet,
Though every drop of water swear against it,
And gape at wid'st to glut him.

VOICES WITHIN Mercy on us! –
We split, we split! – Farewell, my wife and children! –
Farewell, brother! – We split, we split, we split!

ANTONIO Let's all sink wi' th' King.

SEBASTIAN Let's take leave of him.

[*Exeunt Antonio and Sebastian.*

GONZALO Now would I give a thousand furlongs of sea for an acre of barren ground: long heath, brown furze, anything.

The wills above be done, but I would fain die a dry death! [*Exeunt.*

Scene 2. *An Island. Before Prospero's cell.*

Enter PROSPERO *(wearing a cloak and bearing a staff) with* MIRANDA.

MIRANDA If by your art, my dearest father, you have
Put the wild waters in this roar, allay them.
The sky, it seems, would pour down stinking pitch,
But that the sea, mounting to th' welkin's cheek,
Dashes the fire out. O! I have suffered
With those that I saw suffer: a brave vessel
(Who had no doubt some noble creature in her)
Dashed all to pieces: O, the cry did knock
Against my very heart! Poor souls, they perished.
Had I been any god of power, I would
Have sunk the sea within the earth, or ere
It should the good ship so have swallowed and
The fraughting souls within her.

PROSPERO Be collected;
No more amazement: tell your piteous heart
There's no harm done.

MIRANDA O woe the day!

PROSPERO No harm:
I have done nothing but in care of thee
(Of thee, my dear one; thee, my daughter), who
Art ignorant of what thou art, naught knowing
Of whence I am, nor that I am more better
Than Prospero, master of a full poor cell,
And thy no greater father.

MIRANDA More to know
Did never meddle with my thoughts.

PROSPERO 'Tis time
I should inform thee farther. Lend thy hand
And pluck my magic garment from me. – So,
Lie there, my art. – Wipe thou thine eyes, have comfort.
The direful spectacle of the wrack, which touched
The very virtue of compassion in thee,
I have with such provision in mine art
So safely ordered, that there is no soul –
No, not so much perdition as an hair
Betid to any creature in the vessel
Which thou heard'st cry, which thou saw'st sink. Sit down,
For thou must now know farther. [*They sit.*

MIRANDA You have often
Begun to tell me what I am, but stopped,
And left me to a bootless inquisition,
Concluding, 'Stay: not yet.'

PROSPERO The hour's now come;
The very minute bids thee ope thine ear.
Obey, and be attentive. Canst thou remember
A time before we came unto this cell?
I do not think thou canst, for then thou wast not
Our three years old.

MIRANDA Certainly sir, I can.

PROSPERO By what? By any other house, or person?
Of any thing the image, tell me, that
Hath kept with thy remembrance.

MIRANDA 'Tis far off,
And rather like a dream, than an assurance

That my remembrance warrants. Had I not
Four or five women once, that tended me?

PROSPERO Thou hadst; and more, Miranda. But how is it,
That this lives in thy mind? What seest thou else
In the dark backward and abysm of time?
If thou rememb'rest aught ere thou cam'st here,
How thou cam'st here thou mayst.

MIRANDA But that I do not.

PROSPERO Twelve year since, Miranda, twelve year since,
Thy father was the Duke of Millaine and
A prince of power.

MIRANDA Sir, are not you my father?

PROSPERO Thy mother was a piece of virtue, and
She said thou wast my daughter; and thy father
Was Duke of Millaine, and his only heir
A princess, no worse issued.

MIRANDA O the heavens!
What foul play had we, that we came from thence?
Or blessèd was't we did?

PROSPERO Both, both, my girl.
By foul play, as thou sayst, were we heaved thence,
But blessedly holp hither.

MIRANDA O, my heart bleeds
To think o'th' teen that I have turned you to,
Which is from my remembrance. Please you, farther.

PROSPERO My brother, and thy uncle, called Antonio –
I pray thee mark me, that a brother should
Be so perfidious – he, whom next thyself
Of all the world I loved, and to him put
The manage of my state, as at that time
Through all the signories it was the first,

And Prospero the prime duke, being so reputed
In dignity, and for the liberal arts
Without a parallel; those being all my study,
The government I cast upon my brother,
And to my state grew stranger, being transported
And rapt in secret studies. Thy false uncle –
Dost thou attend me?

MIRANDA Sir, most heedfully.

PROSPERO – Being once pérfected how to grant suits,
How to deny them, who t'advance, and who
To trash for over-topping, new created
The creatures that were mine, I say, or changed 'em,
Or else new formed 'em; having both the key
Of officer and office, set all hearts i'th' state
To what tune pleased his ear, that now he was
The ivy which had hid my princely trunk,
And sucked my verdure out on't – Thou attend'st not!

MIRANDA O good sir, I do.

PROSPERO I pray thee mark me. –
I, thus neglecting worldly ends, all dedicated
To closeness and the bettering of my mind
With that which, but by being so retired,
O'er-prized all popular rate, in my false brother
Awaked an evil nature; and my trust,
Like a good parent, did beget of him
A falsehood in its contrary, as great
As my trust was, which had indeed no limit,
A confidence sans bound. He, being thus lorded
Not only with what my revénue yielded
But what my power might else exact, like one
Who having unto truth, by telling of it,
Made such a sinner of his memory

To credit his own lie, he did believe
He was indeed the Duke, out o'th' substitution
And executing th'outward face of royalty
With all prerogative. Hence his ambition growing –
Dost thou hear?

MIRANDA Your tale, sir, would cure deafness.

PROSPERO – To have no screen between this part he played
And him he played it for, he needs will be
Absolute Millaine. Me, poor man, my library
Was dukedom large enough: of temporal royalties
He thinks me now incapable; confederates
(So dry he was for sway) wi'th' King of Naples
To give him annual tribute, do him homage,
Subject his coronet to his crown, and bend
The dukedom yet unbowed (alas, poor Millaine!)
To most ignoble stooping.

MIRANDA O the heavens!

PROSPERO Mark his condition, and th'event; then tell me
If this might be a brother.

MIRANDA I should sin
To think but nobly of my grandmother:
Good wombs have borne bad sons.

PROSPERO Now the condition:
This King of Naples, being an enemy
To me inveterate, hearkens my brother's suit,
Which was that he, in lieu o'th' premises
Of homage, and I know not how much tribute,
Should presently extírpate me and mine
Out of the dukedom, and confer fair Millaine,
With all the honours, on my brother. Whereon,
A treacherous army levied, one midnight,
Fated to th' purpose, did Antonio open

The gates of Millaine, and i'th' dead of darkness
The ministers of th' purpose hurried thence
Me and thy crying self.

MIRANDA Alack, for pity:
I not remembering how I cried out then
Will cry it o'er again: it is a hint
That wrings mine eyes to't.

PROSPERO Hear a little further,
And then I'll bring thee to the present business
Which now's upon's: without the which, this story
Were most impertinent.

MIRANDA Wherefore did they not
That hour destroy us?

PROSPERO Well demanded, wench:
My tale provokes that question. Dear, they durst not,
So dear the love my people bore me; nor set
A mark so bloody on the business; but
With colours fairer painted their fouls ends.
In few, they hurried us aboard a bark,
Bore us some leagues to sea; where they prepared
A rotten carcass of a butt, not rigged,
Nor tackle, sail, nor mast: the very rats
Instinctively have quit it. There they hoist us
To cry to th' sea, that roared to us; to sigh
To th' winds, whose pity, sighing back again,
Did us but loving wrong.

MIRANDA Alack, what trouble
Was I then to you!

PROSPERO O, a cherubin
Thou wast that did preserve me. Thou didst smile,
Infusèd with a fortitude from heaven,
When I have decked the sea with drops full salt,

Under my burthen groaned; which raised in me
An undergoing stomach, to bear up
Against what should ensue.

MIRANDA How came we ashore?

PROSPERO By Providence divine.
Some food we had, and some fresh water, that
A noble Neapolitan, Gonzalo,
Out of his charity, who being then appointed
Master of this design, did give us, with
Rich garments, linens, stuffs, and necessaries
Which since have steaded much. So of his gentleness,
Knowing I loved my books, he furnished me
From mine own library with volumes that
I prize above my dukedom.

MIRANDA Would I might
But ever see that man!

PROSPERO [*rising:*] Now I arise;
Sit still, and hear the last of our sea-sorrow.
[*He dons his mantle.*
Here in this island we arrived, and here
Have I, thy schoolmaster, made thee more profit
Than other princess' can, that have more time
For vainer hours, and tutors not so careful.

MIRANDA Heaven thank you for't. And now, I pray you sir,
For still 'tis beating in my mind, your reason
For raising this sea-storm?

PROSPERO Know thus far forth.
By accident most strange, bountiful Fortune
(Now my dear lady) hath mine enemies
Brought to this shore; and by my prescience
I find my zenith doth depend upon
A most auspicious star, whose influence

If now I court not, but omit, my fortunes
Will ever after droop. Here cease more questions:
Thou art inclined to sleep; 'tis a good dulness,
And give it way: I know thou canst not choose.
[*Miranda sleeps.*
– Come away, servant, come! I am ready now.
Approach, my Ariel. Come!

Enter ARIEL.

ARIEL All hail, great master; grave sir, hail! I come
To answer thy best pleasure: be't to fly,
To swim, to dive into the fire, to ride
On the curled clouds, to thy strong bidding task
Ariel and all his quality.

PROSPERO Hast thou, spirit,
Performed to point the tempest that I bade thee?

ARIEL To every article.
I boarded the King's ship: now on the beak,
Now in the waist, the deck, in every cabin,
I flamed amazement. Sometimes I 'd divide
And burn in many places: on the topmast,
The yards and boresprit would I flame distinctly,
Then meet and join. Jove's lightning, the precursors
O'th' dreadful thunder-claps, more momentary
And sight-outrunning were not; the fire and cracks
Of sulphurous roaring the most mighty Neptune
Seem to besiege, and make his bold waves tremble,
Yea, his dread trident shake.

PROSPERO My brave spirit!
Who was so firm, so constant, that this coil
Would not infect his reason?

ARIEL Not a soul

But felt a fever of the mad, and played
Some tricks of desperation; all but mariners
Plunged in the foaming brine, and quit the vessel,
Then all afire with me: the King's son Ferdinand,
With hair up-staring (then like reeds, not hair),
Was the first man that leapt; cried 'Hell is empty,
And all the devils are here!'

PROSPERO Why, that's my spirit!
But was not this nigh shore?

ARIEL Close by, my master.

PROSPERO But are they, Ariel, safe?

ARIEL Not a hair perished:
On their sustaining garments not a blemish,
But fresher than before; and, as thou bad'st me,
In troops I have dispersed them 'bout the isle.
The King's son have I landed by himself,
Whom I left cooling of the air with sighs,
In an odd angle of the isle, and sitting,
His arms in this sad knot.

PROSPERO Of the King's ship,
The mariners, say how thou hast disposed,
And all the rest o'th' fleet.

ARIEL Safely in harbour
Is the King's ship: in the deep nook, where once
Thou called'st me up at midnight to fetch dew
From the still-vexed Bermoothès, there she's hid;
The mariners all under hatches stowed,
Who, with a charm joined to their suffered labour,
I have left asleep; and for the rest o'th' fleet,
Which I dispersed, they all have met again,
And are upon the Mediterranean flote
Bound sadly home for Naples,

Supposing that they saw the King's ship wracked,
And his great person perish.

PROSPERO Ariel, thy charge
Exactly is performed; but there's more work.
What is the time o'th' day?

ARIEL Past the mid-season.

PROSPERO At least two glasses. The time 'twixt six and now
Must by us both be spent most preciously.

ARIEL Is there more toil? Since thou dost give me pains,
Let me remember thee what thou hast promised,
Which is not yet performed me.

PROSPERO How now? Moody?
What is't thou canst demand?

ARIEL My liberty.

PROSPERO Before the time be out? No more!

ARIEL I prithee,
Remember I have done thee worthy service,
Told thee no lies, made no mistakings, served
Without or grudge or grumblings; thou didst promise
To bate me a full year.

PROSPERO Dost thou forget
From what a torment I did free thee?

ARIEL No.

PROSPERO Thou dost, and think'st it much to tread the ooze
Of the salt deep,
To run upon the sharp wind of the north,
To do me business in the veins o'th'earth
When it is baked with frost.

ARIEL I do not, sir.

PROSPERO Thou liest, malignant thing! Hast thou forgot
The foul witch Sycorax, who with age and envy
Was grown into a hoop? Hast thou forgot her?

ARIEL No, sir.

PROSPERO Thou hast. Where was she born? Speak: tell me.

ARIEL Sir, in Argier.

PROSPERO O, was she so? I must
Once in month recount what thou hast been,
Which thou forget'st. This damned witch Sycorax,
For mischiefs manifold, and sorceries terrible
To enter human hearing, from Argier
Thou know'st was banished; for one thing she did
They would not take her life. Is not this true?

ARIEL Ay, sir.

PROSPERO This blue-eyed hag was hither brought with child,
And here was left by th' sailors. Thou, my slave,
As thou report'st thyself, was then her servant,
And for thou wast a spirit too delicate
To act her earthy and abhorred commands,
Refusing her grand hests, she did confine thee,
By help of her more potent ministers,
And in her most unmitigable rage,
Into a cloven pine: within which rift
Imprisoned, thou didst painfully remain
A dozen years: within which space she died,
And left thee there: where thou didst vent thy groans
As fast as mill-wheels strike. Then was this island
(Save for the son that she did litter here,
A freckled whelp, hag-born) not honoured with
A human shape.

ARIEL Yes: Caliban her son.

PROSPERO Dull thing, I say so: he, that Caliban
Whom now I keep in service. Thou best know'st
What torment I did find thee in: thy groans

Did make wolves howl, and penetrate the breasts
Of ever-angry bears; it was a torment
To lay upon the damned, which Sycorax
Could not again undo. It was mine art,
When I arrived and heard thee, that made gape
The pine, and let thee out.

ARIEL I thank thee, master.

PROSPERO If thou more murmur'st, I will rend an oak
And peg thee in his knotty entrails till
Thou hast howled away twelve winters.

ARIEL Pardon, master.
I will be correspondent to command,
And do my spriting gently.

PROSPERO Do so: and after two days
I will discharge thee.

ARIEL That's my noble master!
What shall I do? Say what: what shall I do?

PROSPERO Go make thyself like a nymph o'th' sea; be subject
To no sight but thine and mine, invisible
To every eye-ball else: go take this shape,
And hither come in't. Go: hence,
With diligence. [*Exit Ariel.*
– Awake, dear heart, awake, thou hast slept well;
Awake.

MIRANDA The strangeness of your story put
Heaviness in me.

PROSPERO Shake it off. Come on;
We'll visit Caliban, my slave, who never
Yields us kind answer.

MIRANDA 'Tis a villain, sir,
I do not love to look on.

PROSPERO But, as 'tis,

We cannot miss him: he does make our fire,
Fetch in our wood, and serves in offices
That profit us. – What ho! Slave! Caliban!
Thou earth, thou! Speak.

CALIBAN [*within:*] There's wood enough within.

PROSPERO Come forth, I say; there's other business for thee.
Come, thou tortoise, when?

Enter ARIEL *like a water-nymph.*

Fine apparition! My quaint Ariel,
Hark in thine ear. [*He whispers.*]

ARIEL My lord, it shall be done. [*Exit.*

PROSPERO [*to Caliban:*] Thou poisonous slave, got by the devil himself
Upon thy wicked dam: come forth.

Enter CALIBAN.

CALIBAN As wicked dew as e'er my mother brushed
With raven's feather from unwholesome fen
Drop on you both! A south-west blow on ye,
And blister you all o'er!

PROSPERO For this, be sure, tonight thou shalt have cramps,
Side-stitches that shall pen thy breath up; urchins
Shall, for that vast of night that they may work,
All exercise on thee: thou shalt be pinched
As thick as honeycomb, each pinch more stinging
Than bees had made 'em.

CALIBAN I must eat my dinner.
This island's mine, by Sycorax my mother,
Which thou tak'st from me. When thou cam'st first,
Thou strok'st me, and made much of me; wouldst give me

Water with berries in't, and teach me how
To name the bigger light, and how the less,
That burn by day and night: and then I loved thee,
And showed thee all the qualities o'th'isle,
The fresh springs, brine-pits, barren place and fertile.
Curst be I that did so! All the charms
Of Sycorax, toads, beetles, bats, light on you:
For I am all the subjects that you have,
Which first was mine own king; and here you sty me
In this hard rock, whiles you do keep from me
The rest o'th'island.

PROSPERO Thou most lying slave,
Whom stripes may move, not kindness! I have used thee
(Filth as thou art) with húmane care, and lodged thee
In mine own cell, till thou didst seek to violate
The honour of my child.

CALIBAN O ho, O ho! Would't had been done!
Thou didst prevent me; I had peopled else
This isle with Calibans.

MIRANDA Abhorrèd slave,
Which any print of goodness will not take,
Being capable of all ill! I pitied thee,
Took pains to make thee speak, taught thee each hour
One thing or other: when thou didst not, savage,
Know thine own meaning, but wouldst gabble like
A thing most brutish, I endowed thy purposes
With words that made them known. But thy vile race,
Though thou didst learn, had that in't which good natures
Could not abide to be with; therefore wast thou
Deservedly confined into this rock,

Who hadst deserved more than a prison.

CALIBAN You taught me language, and my profit on't
Is, I know how to curse: the red plague rid you,
For learning me your language.

PROSPERO Hag-seed, hence!
Fetch us in fuel, and be quick – thou'rt best –
To answer other business. Shrug'st thou, Malice?
If thou neglect'st or dost unwillingly
What I command, I'll rack thee with old cramps,
Fill all thy bones with achès, make thee roar,
That beasts shall tremble at thy din.

CALIBAN No, pray thee.
[*Aside:*] I must obey; his art is of such power,
It would control my dam's god Setebos,
And make a vassal of him.

PROSPERO So, slave, hence!
[*Exit Caliban.*

Enter ARIEL, *invisible to others, playing and singing,*
FERDINAND *following. Prospero and Miranda stand aside.*

ARIEL [*sings:*] Come unto these yellow sands,
And then take hands;
Curtsied when you have and kissed
(The wild waves whist),
Foot it featly here and there,
And, sweet sprites, bear
The burthen.

SPIRITS [*dispersedly within:*]
Hark, hark!
'Bow-wow!'
The watch dogs bark:
'Bow-wow!'

ARIEL Hark, hark:
I hear
The strain of strutting Chanticleer
Cry 'Cockadiddle-dow!'

FERDINAND Where should this music be? I'th'air, or th'earth?
It sounds no more; and sure it waits upon
Some god o'th'island. Sitting on a bank,
Weeping again the King my father's wrack,
This music crept by me upon the waters,
Allaying both their fury and my passion
With its sweet air: thence I have followed it
(Or it hath drawn me rather); but 'tis gone.
No, it begins again.

ARIEL [*sings:*] Full fathom five thy father lies.
Of his bones are coral made;
Those are pearls that were his eyes;
Nothing of him that doth fade,
But doth suffer a sea-change
Into something rich and strange.
Sea-nymphs hourly ring his knell.

SPIRITS [*within:*] Ding-dong.

ARIEL [*sings:*] Hark: now I hear them: ding-dong bell.

FERDINAND The ditty does remember my drowned father.
[*Music.*] This is no mortal business, nor no sound
That the earth owes: I hear it now above me.

PROSPERO [*to Miranda:*] The fringèd curtains of thine eye advance,
And say what thou seest yond.

MIRANDA What is't? A spirit?
Lord, how it looks about. Believe me, sir,
It carries a brave form. But 'tis a spirit.

PROSPERO No, wench; it eats and sleeps, and hath such senses

As we have, such. This gallant which thou seest
Was in the wrack; and but he's something stained
With grief (that's beauty's canker), thou mightst call him
A goodly person. He hath lost his fellows,
And strays about to find 'em.

MIRANDA I might call him
A thing divine, for nothing natural
I ever saw so noble.

PROSPERO [*aside:*] It goes on, I see,
As my soul prompts it. [*To Ariel:*] Spirit, fine spirit, I'll free thee
Within two days for this.

FERDINAND [*seeing Miranda:*] Most sure, the goddess
On whom these airs attend! – Vouchsafe my prayer
May know if you remain upon this island,
And that you will some good instruction give
How I may bear me here. My prime request,
Which I do last pronounce, is – O you wonder! –
If you be maid, or no?

MIRANDA No wonder, sir,
But certainly a maid.

FERDINAND My language? Heavens!
I am the best of them that speak this speech,
Were I but where 'tis spoken.

PROSPERO How? The best?
What wert thou if the King of Naples heard thee?

FERDINAND A single thing, as I am now, that wonders
To hear thee speak of Naples. He does hear me,
And that he does, I weep: myself am Naples,
Who with mine eyes, never since at ebb, beheld

The King my father wracked.

MIRANDA Alack, for mercy!

FERDINAND Yes, faith, and all his lords, the Duke of Millaine
And his brave son being twain.

PROSPERO [*aside:*] The Duke of Millaine
And his more braver daughter could control thee,
If now 'twere fit to do't. At the first sight
They have changed eyes. – Delicate Ariel,
I'll set thee free for this. [*To Ferdinand:*] A word, good sir.
I fear you have done yourself some wrong; a word.

MIRANDA Why speaks my father so ungently? This
Is the third man that ever I saw; the first
That e'er I sighed for. Pity move my father
To be inclined my way.

FERDINAND O, if a virgin,
And your affection not gone forth, I'll make you
The Queen of Naples.

PROSPERO Soft, sir: one word more.
[*Aside:*]They are both in either's powers; but this swift business
I must uneasy make, lest too light winning
Make the prize light.[*To Ferdinand:*] One word more: I charge thee
That thou attend me. Thou dost here usurp
The name thou ow'st not, and hast put thyself
Upon this island as a spy, to win it
From me, the lord on't.

FERDINAND No, as I am a man.

MIRANDA There's nothing ill can dwell in such a temple.

If the ill spirit have so fair a house,
Good things will strive to dwell with't.

PROSPERO [*to Ferdinand:*] Follow me.
[*To Miranda:*] Speak not you for him: he's a traitor.
[*To Ferdinand:*] Come:
I'll manacle thy neck and feet together;
Sea-water shalt thou drink; thy food shall be
The fresh-brook mussels, withered roots, and husks
Wherein the acorn cradled. Follow.

FERDINAND No:
I will resist such entertainment till
Mine enemy has more power.
[*He draws his sword, but is paralysed by Prospero's magic.*

MIRANDA O dear father,
Make not too rash a trial of him, for
He's gentle, and not fearful.

PROSPERO What, I say,
My foot my tutor? – Put thy sword up, traitor,
Who mak'st a show, but dar'st not strike, thy conscience
Is so possessed with guilt. Come from thy ward,
For I can here disarm thee with this stick,
And make thy weapon drop.
[*Ferdinand's sword falls from his hand.*

MIRANDA Beseech you, father.

PROSPERO Hence! Hang not on my garments.

MIRANDA Sir, have pity;
I'll be his surety.

PROSPERO Silence. One word more
Shall make me chide thee, if not hate thee. What,
An advocate for an impostor? Hush!

Thou think'st there is no more such shapes as he,
Having seen but him and Caliban. Foolish wench,
To th' most of men, this is a Caliban,
And they to him are angels.

MIRANDA My affections
Are then most humble: I have no ambition
To see a goodlier man.

PROSPERO [*to Ferdinand:*] Come on, obey:
Thy nerves are in their infancy again,
And have no vigour in them.

FERDINAND So they are:
My spirits, as in a dream, are all bound up.
My father's loss, the weakness which I feel,
The wrack of all my friends, nor this man's threats,
To whom I am subdued, are but light to me,
Might I but through my prison once a day
Behold this maid. All corners else o'th'earth
Let liberty make use of; space enough
Have I in such a prison.

PROSPERO [*aside:*] It works.
[*To Ferdinand:*] Come on.
[*To Ariel:*] Thou hast done well, fine Ariel.
[*To Ferdinand:*] Follow me.
[*To Ariel:*] Hark what thou else shalt do me.

MIRANDA [*to Ferdinand:*] Be of comfort;
My father's of a better nature, sir,
Than he appears by speech: this is unwonted
Which now came from him.

PROSPERO [*to Ariel:*] Thou shalt be as free
As mountain winds; but then exactly do
All points of my command.

ARIEL To th' syllable.

PROSPERO [*to Ferdinand:*] Come, follow.
[*To Miranda:*] Speak not for him.
[*Exeunt.*

ACT 2

Scene 1. *Another part of the island.*

Enter ALONSO, SEBASTIAN, ANTONIO, GONZALO, ADRIAN *and* FRANCISCO.

GONZALO [*to Alonso*:] Beseech you, sir, be merry; you have cause,
So have we all, of joy; for our escape
Is much beyond our loss. Our hint of woe
Is common; every day some sailor's wife,
The masters of some merchant, and the merchant,
Have just our theme of woe. But for the miracle –
I mean our preservation – few in millions
Can speak like us: then wisely, good sir, weigh
Our sorrow with our comfort.

ALONSO Prithee, peace.

SEBASTIAN [*to Antonio:*] He receives comfort like cold porridge.

ANTONIO The visitor will not give him o'er so.

SEBASTIAN Look, he's winding up the watch of his wit; by and by it will strike.

GONZALO [*to Alonso:*] Sir –

SEBASTIAN [*to Antonio:*] One: tell.

GONZALO When every grief is entertained that's offered,
Comes to the entertainer –

SEBASTIAN [*aloud:*] A dollar.

GONZALO Dolour comes to him indeed: you have spoken truer than you purposed.

SEBASTIAN You have taken it wiselier than I meant you should.

GONZALO [*to Alonso:*] Therefore, my lord, –

ANTONIO [*to Sebastian:*] Fie, what a spendthrift is he of his tongue.

ALONSO [*to Gonzalo:*] I prithee, spare.

GONZALO Well, I have done; but yet –

SEBASTIAN [*to Antonio:*] He will be talking.

ANTONIO Which, of he or Adrian, – for a good wager – first begins to crow?

SEBASTIAN The old cock.

ANTONIO The cockerel.

SEBASTIAN Done, The wager?

ANTONIO A laughter.

SEBASTIAN A match!

ADRIAN [*to Gonzalo:*] Though this island seem to be desert, –

ANTONIO Ha, ha, ha!

SEBASTIAN So, you're paid.

ADRIAN Uninhabitable, and almost inaccessible, –

SEBASTIAN Yet –

ADRIAN Yet –

ANTONIO He could not miss't.

ADRIAN It must needs be of subtle, tender and delicate temperance.

ANTONIO 'Temperance' was a delicate wench.

SEBASTIAN Ay, and a subtle, as he most learnedly delivered.

ADRIAN The air breathes upon us here most sweetly.

SEBASTIAN As if it had lungs, and rotten ones.

ANTONIO Or, as ’twere perfumed by a fen.

GONZALO Here is every thing advantageous to life.

ANTONIO Or, as ’twere perfumed by a fen.

GONZALO Here is every thing advantageous to life.

ANTONIO True, save means to live.

SEBASTIAN Of that there’s none, or little.

GONZALO How lush and lusty the grass looks! How green!

ANTONIO The ground, indeed, is tawny.

SEBASTIAN With an eye of green in’t.

ANTONIO He misses not much.

SEBASTIAN No: he doth but mistake the truth totally.

GONZALO But the rarity of it is, which is indeed almost beyond credit, –

SEBASTIAN As many vouched rarities are.

GONZALO That our garments, being, as they were, drenched in the sea, hold notwithstanding their freshness and glosses, being rather new-dyed than stained with salt water.

ANTONIO If but one of his pockets could speak, would it not say he lies?

SEBASTIAN Ay, or very falsely pocket up his report.

GONZALO Methinks our garments are now as fresh as when we put them on first in Afric, at the marriage of the King’s fair daughter Claribel to the King of Tunis.

SEBASTIAN ’Twas a sweet marriage, and we prosper well in our return.

ADRIAN Tunis was never graced before with such a paragon to their queen.

GONZALO Not since widow Dido’s time.

ANTONIO [*to Sebastian:*] ‘Widow’? A pox o’that! How came that ‘widow’ in? ‘Widow Dido’!

SEBASTIAN What if he had said 'widower Aeneas' too? Good Lord, how you take it!

ADRIAN [*to Gonzalo:*] Widow Dido, said you? You make me study of that: she was of Carthage, not of Tunis.

GONZALO This Tunis, sir, was Carthage.

ADRIAN Carthage?

GONZALO I assure you, Carthage.

ANTONIO [*to Sebastian:*] His word is more than the miraculous harp.

SEBASTIAN He hath raised the wall, and houses too.

ANTONIO What impossible matter will he make easy next?

SEBASTIAN I think he will carry this island home in his pocket, and give it his son for an apple.

ANTONIO And, sowing the kernels of it in the sea, bring forth more islands.

GONZALO [*to Adrian:*] Ay.

ANTONIO [*to Sebastian:*] Why, in good time.

GONZALO [*to Alonso:*] Sir, we were talking, that our garments seem now as fresh as when we were at Tunis at the marriage of your daughter, who is now queen.

ANTONIO And the rarest that e'er came there.

SEBASTIAN Bate, I beseech you, widow Dido.

ANTONIO O, widow Dido! Ay, widow Dido.

GONZALO [*to Alonso:*] Is not, sir, my doublet as fresh as the first day I wore it – I mean, in a sort –

ANTONIO [*to Sebastian:*] That sort was well fished for.

GONZALO When I wore it at your daughter's marriage?

ALONSO You cram these words into mine ears, against
The stomach of my sense. Would I had never
Married my daughter there: for, coming thence,
My son is lost; and, in my rate, she too,
Who is so far from Italy removed,

I ne'er again shall see her. O thou mine heir
Of Naples and of Millaine, what strange fish
Hath made his meal on thee?

FRANCISCO Sir, he may live.
I saw him beat the surges under him,
And ride upon their backs; he trod the water,
Whose enmity he flung aside, and breasted
The surge most swoll'n that met him; his bold head
'Bove the contentious waves he kept, and oared
Himself with his good arms in lusty stroke
To th' shore, that o'er his wave-worn basis bowed,
As stooping to relieve him. I not doubt
He came alive to land.

ALONSO No, no; he's gone.

SEBASTIAN Sir, you may thank yourself for this great loss,
That would not bless our Europe with your daughter,
But rather lose her to an African,
Where she, at least, is banished from your eye,
Who hath cause to wet the grief on't.

ALONSO Prithee, peace.

SEBASTIAN You were kneeled to and impórtuned otherwise
By all of us: and the fair soul herself
Weighed between loathness and obedience, at
Which end o'th' beam should bow. We have lost your son,
I fear, for ever. Millaine and Naples have
Mo widows in them of this business' making
Than we bring men to comfort them:
The fault's your own.

ALONSO So is the dear'st o'th' loss.

GONZALO My lord Sebastian,
The truth you speak doth lack some gentleness,

And time to speak it in: you rub the sore,
When you should bring the plaster.

SEBASTIAN Very well.

ANTONIO And most chirurgeonly.

GONZALO [*to Alonso:*] It is foul weather in us all, good sir,
When you are cloudy.

SEBASTIAN Fowl weather?

ANTONIO Very foul.

GONZALO [*to Alonso:*] Had I plantation of this isle, my lord, –

ANTONIO He'd sow't with nettle-seed.

SEBASTIAN Or docks, or mallows.

GONZALO And were the king on't, what would I do?

SEBASTIAN Scape being drunk, for want of wine.

GONZALO I'th' commonwealth I would by contraries
Execute all things: for no kind of traffic
Would I admit; no name of magistrate;
Letters should not be known; riches, poverty,
And use of service, none; contract, succession,
Bourn, bound of land, tilth, vineyard, none;
No use of metal, corn, or wine, or oil;
No occupation, all men idle, all,
And women too, but innocent and pure;
No sovereignty –

SEBASTIAN Yet he would be king on't.

ANTONIO The latter end of his commonwealth forgets the
beginning.

GONZALO All things in common nature should produce
Without sweat or endeavour. Treason, felony,
Sword, pike, knife, gun, or need of any engine,
Would I not have; but nature should bring forth,
Of it own kind, all foison, all abundance,
To feed my innocent people.

SEBASTIAN [*to Antonio:*] No marrying 'mong his subjects?

ANTONIO None, man, all idle: whores and knaves.

GONZALO [*to Alonso:*] I would with such perfection govern, sir,
T'excel the Golden Age.

SEBASTIAN God save his Majesty!

ANTONIO Long live Gonzalo!

GONZALO And – do you mark me, sir?

ALONSO Prithee, no more: thou dost talk nothing to me.

GONZALO I do well believe your Highness, and did it to minister occasion to these gentlemen, who are of such sensible and nimble lungs, that they always use to laugh at nothing.

ANTONIO 'Twas you we laughed at.

GONZALO Who, in this kind of merry fooling, am nothing to you: so you may continue, and laugh at nothing still.

ANTONIO What a blow was there given!

SEBASTIAN An it had not fallen flat-long.

GONZALO You are gentlemen of brave mettle: you would lift the moon out of her sphere, if she would continue in it five weeks without changing.

Enter ARIEL, *invisible to them, playing solemn music.*

SEBASTIAN We would so, and then go a-batfowling.

ANTONIO [*to Gonzalo:*] Nay, good my lord, be not angry.

GONZALO No, I warrant you. I will not adventure my discretion so weakly. Will you laugh me asleep? For I am very heavy.

ANTONIO Go sleep, and hear us.

[*Gonzalo, Adrian and Francisco sleep.*

ALONSO What, all so soon asleep? I wish mine eyes
Would, with themselves, shut up my thoughts. I find
They are inclined to do so.

SEBASTIAN Please you, sir,
Do not omit the heavy offer of it:
It seldom visits sorrow; when it doth,
It is a comforter.

ANTONIO We two, my lord,
Will guard your person while you take your rest,
And watch your safety.

ALONSO Thank you. Wondrous heavy.
[*Alonso sleeps. Exit Ariel.*

SEBASTIAN What a strange drowsiness possesses them!

ANTONIO It is the quality o'th' climate.

SEBASTIAN Why
Doth it not then our eyelids sink? I find not
Myself disposed to sleep.

ANTONIO Nor I; my spirits are nimble.
They fell together all, as by consent;
They dropped, as by a thunder-stroke. What might,
Worthy Sebastian, O what might – ? No more.
And yet, methinks, I see it in thy face,
What thou shouldst be: th'occasion speaks thee, and
My strong imagination sees a crown
Dropping upon thy head.

SEBASTIAN What? Art thou waking?

ANTONIO Do you not hear me speak?

SEBASTIAN I do, and surely
It is a sleepy language, and thou speak'st
Out of thy sleep. What is it thou didst say?
This is a strange repose, to be asleep
With eyes wide open; standing, speaking, moving,
And yet so fast asleep.

ANTONIO Noble Sebastian,
Thou let'st thy fortune sleep – die rather; wink'st

Whiles thou art waking.

SEBASTIAN Thou dost snore distinctly;
There's meaning in thy snores.

ANTONIO I am more serious than my custom. You
Must be so too, if heed me: which to do,
Trebles thee o'er.

SEBASTIAN Well: I am standing water.

ANTONIO I'll teach you how to flow.

SEBASTIAN Do so; to ebb,
Hereditary sloth instructs me.

ANTONIO O,
If you but knew how you the purpose cherish
Whiles thus you mock it; how, in stripping it,
You more invest it! Ebbing men, indeed,
Most often, do so near the bottom run
By their own fear, or sloth.

SEBASTIAN Prithee, say on.
The setting of thine eye and cheek proclaim
A matter from thee, and a birth, indeed,
Which throes thee much to yield.

ANTONIO Thus, sir:
Although this lord of weak remembrance, this,
Who shall be of as little memory
When he is earthed, hath here almost persuaded
(For he's a spirit of persuasion, only
Professes to persuade) the King his son's alive,
'Tis as impossible that he's undrowned,
As he that sleeps here swims.

SEBASTIAN I have no hope
That he's undrowned.

ANTONIO O, out of that 'no hope',
What great hope have you! No hope, that way, is

Another way so high an hope, that even
Ambition cannot pierce a wink beyond,
But doubt discovery there. Will you grant with me
That Ferdinand is drowned?

SEBASTIAN He's gone.

ANTONIO Then, tell me,
Who's the next heir of Naples?

SEBASTIAN Claribel.

ANTONIO She that is Queen of Tunis: she that dwells
Ten leagues beyond man's life: she that from Naples
Can have no note (unless the sun were post:
The man i'th' moon's too slow) till new-born chins
Be rough and razorable; she that from whom
We all were sea-swallowed, though some cast again
(And that by destiny) to perform an act,
Whereof what's past is prologue; what to come,
In yours and my discharge.

SEBASTIAN What stuff is this? How say you?
'Tis true, my brother's daughter's Queen of Tunis;
So is she heir of Naples; 'twixt which regions
There is some space.

ANTONIO A space whose every cubit
Seems to cry out, 'How shall that Claribel
Measure us back to Naples? Keep in Tunis,
And let Sebastian wake.' Say this were death
That now hath seized them – why, they were no worse
Than now they are. There be that can rule Naples
As well as he that sleeps; lords, that can prate
As amply and unnecessarily
As this Gonzalo: I myself could make
A chough of as deep chat. O, that you bore

The mind that I do; what a sleep were this
For your advancement! Do you understand me?

SEBASTIAN Methinks I do.

ANTONIO And how does your content
Tender your own good fortune?

SEBASTIAN I remember
You did supplant your brother Prospero.

ANTONIO True;
And look how well my garments sit upon me,
Much feater than before. My brother's servants
Were then my fellows; now they are my men.

SEBASTIAN But, for your conscience?

ANTONIO Ay, sir: Where lies that? If 'twere a kibe,
'Twould put me to my slipper; but I feel not
This deity in my bosom. Twenty consciences,
That stand 'twixt me and Millaine, candied be they,
And melt ere they molest! Here lies your brother,
No better than the earth he lies upon,
If he were that which now he's like – that's dead;
Whom I with this obedient steel, three inches of it,
Can lay to bed for ever; whiles you, doing thus,
To the perpetual wink for aye might put
This ancient morsel, this Sir Prudence, who
Should not upbraid our course. For all the rest,
They'll take suggestion as a cat laps milk;
They'll tell the clock to any business that
We say befits the hour.

SEBASTIAN Thy case, dear friend,
Shall be my precedent: as thou got'st Millaine,
I'll come by Naples. Draw thy sword. One stroke
Shall free thee from the tribute which thou payest,
And I the King shall love thee.

ANTONIO Draw together;
And when I rear my hand, do you the like
To fall it on Gonzalo. [*They draw their swords.*

SEBASTIAN O, but one word.

[*They talk apart.*

Music. Enter ARIEL, *unseen by them.*

ARIEL [*to Gonzalo:*] My master, through his art, foresees the danger
That you, his friend, are in, and sends me forth
(For else his project dies) to keep them living.
[*He sings in Gonzalo's ear:*]
While you here do snoring lie,
Open-eyed conspiracy
His time doth take.
If of life you keep a care,
Shake off slumber, and beware.
Awake! Awake!

ANTONIO [*to Sebastian:*] Then let us both be sudden.

GONZALO [*waking:*] Now, good angels
Preserve the King! [*The others wake.*

ALONSO Why, how now? Ho! Awake! Why are you drawn?
Wherefore this ghastly looking?

GONZALO What's the matter?

SEBASTIAN Whiles we stood here securing your repose,
Even now, we heard a hollow burst of bellowing,
Like bulls, or rather lions: did't not wake you?
It struck mine ear most terribly.

ALONSO I heard nothing.

ANTONIO O, 'twas a din to fright a monster's ear –
To make an earthquake! Sure, it was the roar
Of a whole herd of lions.

ALONSO Heard you this, Gonzalo?

GONZALO Upon mine honour, sir, I heard a humming –
And that a strange one too – which did awake me.
I shaked you, sir, and cried. As mine eyes opened,
I saw their weapons drawn. There was a noise,
That's verily. 'Tis best we stand upon our guard,
Or that we quit this place. Let's draw our weapons.

ALONSO Lead off this ground, and let's make further search
For my poor son.

GONZALO Heavens keep him from these beasts;
For he is, sure, i'th'island.

ALONSO Lead away.

[*Exeunt all but Ariel.*

ARIEL Prospero, my lord, shall know what I have done.
So, King, go safely on to seek thy son.

[*Exit.*

Scene 2. *Another part of the island.*

Enter CALIBAN, *with a burden of wood. Thunder heard.*

CALIBAN All the infections that the sun sucks up
From bogs, fens, flats, on Prosper fall, and make him
By inch-meal a disease! [*Thunder.*] His spirits hear me,
And yet I needs must curse. But they'll nor pinch,
Fright me with urchin-shows, pitch me i'th' mire,
Nor lead me, like a firebrand in the dark,
Out of my way, unless he bid 'em; but
For every trifle are they set upon me:
Sometime like apes, that mow and chatter at me,
And after bite me; then like hedgehogs, which
Lie tumbling in my barefoot way, and mount

Their pricks at my footfall; sometime am I
All wound with adders, who with cloven tongues
Do hiss me into madness –

Enter TRINCULO.

Lo, now, lo!
Here comes a spirit of his, and to torment me
For bringing wood in slowly. I'll fall flat.
Perchance he will not mind me. [*He lies concealed beneath his gaberdine.*

TRINCULO Here's neither bush nor shrub to bear off any weather at all, and another storm brewing. I hear it sing i'th' wind. Yond same black cloud, yond huge one, looks like a foul bombard that would shed his liquor. If it should thunder, as it did before, I know not where to hide my head: yond same cloud cannot choose but fall by pailfuls. [*He sees Caliban.*] What have we here? A man or a fish? Dead or alive? A fish, he smells like a fish; a very ancient and fish-like smell; a kind of not-of-the-newest poor-John: a strange fish. Were I in England now (as once I was), and had but this fish painted, not a holiday fool there but would give a piece of silver: there would this monster make a man. Any strange beast there makes a man: when they will not give a doit to relieve a lame beggar, they will lay out ten to see a dead Indian. Legged like a man; and his fins like arms. Warm, o' my troth! I do now let loose my opinion, hold it no longer: this is no fish, but an islander, that hath lately suffered by a thunderbolt. [*Thunder.*] Alas, the storm is come again. My best way is to creep under his gabardine: there is no other shelter hereabout. Misery acquaints a man with strange bed-fellows. I will here shroud till the dregs of the storm be past.

He hides. Enter STEPHANO, *singing; a wooden bottle in his hand.*

STEPHANO
I shall no more to sea, to sea;
Here shall I die ashore, –
This is a very scurvy tune to sing at a man's funeral:
Well, here's my comfort. [*He drinks.*
[*He sings:*]
The master, the swabber, the boatswain, and I,
The gunner, and his mate,
Loved Mall, Meg, and Marian, and Margery,
But none of us cared for Kate;
For she had a tongue with a tang,
Would cry to a sailor, 'Go hang!'
She loved not the savour of tar nor of pitch,
Yet a tailor might scratch her where'er she did itch.
Then to sea, boys, and let her go hang!
This is a scurvy tune too: but here's my comfort. [*He drinks.*

CALIBAN [*to Trinculo:*] Do not torment me! O!

STEPHANO What's the matter? Have we devils here? Do you put tricks upon's with salvages and men of Inde, ha? I have not scaped drowning to be afeard now of your four legs: for it hath been said: 'As proper a man as ever went on four legs cannot make him give ground'; and it shall be said so again, while Stephano breathes at nostrils.

CALIBAN The spirit torments me! O!

STEPHANO This is some monster of the isle, with four legs; who hath got, as I take it, an ague. Where the devil should he learn our language? I will give him some relief, if it be but for that. If I can recover him, and keep him tame, and get to Naples with him, he's a present for any emperor that ever trod on neat's-leather.

CALIBAN Do not torment me, prithee! I'll bring my wood home faster.

STEPHANO He's in his fit now, and does not talk after the wisest. He shall taste of my bottle: if he have never drunk wine afore, it will go near to remove his fit. If I can recover him, and keep him tame, I will not take too much for him; he shall pay for him that hath him, and that soundly.

CALIBAN Thou dost me yet but little hurt; thou wilt anon, I know it by thy trembling. Now Prosper works upon thee.

STEPHANO Come on your ways: open your mouth: here is that which will give language to you, cat. Open your mouth; this will shake your shaking, I can tell you, and that soundly. [*Caliban drinks, but flinches.*] You cannot tell who's your friend; open your chaps again.

TRINCULO I should know that voice. It should be – but he is drowned; and these are devils; O, defend me!

STEPHANO Four legs and two voices: a most delicate monster. His forward voice now is to speak well of his friend; his backward voice is to utter foul speeches, and to detract. If all the wine in my bottle will recover him, I will help his ague. Come. [*Caliban drinks again.*] Amen. I will pour some in thy other mouth.

TRINCULO Stephano!

STEPHANO Doth thy other mouth call me? Mercy, mercy! This is a devil, and no monster: I will leave him – I have no long spoon.

TRINCULO Stephano! If thou beest Stephano, touch me, and speak to me: for I am Trinculo – be not afeard – thy good friend Trinculo.

STEPHANO If thou beest Trinculo, come forth. I'll pull thee by the lesser legs. If any be Trinculo's legs, these are they. [*Trinculo emerges.*] Thou art very Trinculo, indeed! How cam'st thou to be the siege of this moon-calf? Can he vent Trinculos?

TRINCULO [*rising:*] I took him to be killed with a thunder-stroke. But art thou not drowned, Stephano? I hope now, thou art not drowned. Is the storm overblown? I hid me under the dead moon-calf's gabardine, for fear of the storm. And art thou living, Stephano? O Stephano, two Neapolitans scaped!

STEPHANO Prithee do not turn me about, my stomach is not constant.

CALIBAN [*aside:*] These be fine things, and if they be not sprites!
That's a brave god, and bears celestial liquor:
I will kneel to him. [*Caliban kneels.*

STEPHANO [*to Trinculo:*] How didst thou scape? How cam'st thou hither? Swear by this bottle, how thou cam'st hither. I escaped upon a butt of sack which the sailors heaved o'er-board – by this bottle, which I made of the bark of a tree with mine own hands since I was cast ashore.

CALIBAN I'll swear upon that bottle to be thy true subject, for the liquor is not earthly.

STEPHANO [*to Trinculo:*] Here; swear then how thou escaped'st.

TRINCULO Swam ashore, man, like a duck. I can swim like a duck, I'll be sworn.

STEPHANO Here, kiss the book. [*Trinculo drinks.*] Though thou canst swim like a duck, thou art made like a goose.

TRINCULO O Stephano, hast any more of this?

STEPHANO The whole butt, man. My cellar is in a rock by th' sea-side, where my wine is hid. [*To Caliban:*] How now, moon-calf? How does thine ague?

CALIBAN Hast thou not dropped from heaven?

STEPHANO Out o'th' moon, I do assure thee. I was the man i'th' moon, when time was.

CALIBAN I have seen thee in her, and I do adore thee. My mistress showed me thee, and thy dog and thy bush.

STEPHANO Come, swear to that: kiss the book. I will furnish it anon with new contents. Swear. [*Rising, Caliban drinks.*

TRINCULO By this good light, this is a very shallow monster! I afeard of him? A very weak monster. 'The man i'th' moon'! A most poor credulous monster. [*Caliban empties bottle.*] Well drawn, monster, in good sooth.

CALIBAN I'll show thee every fertile inch of the island;
And I will kiss thy foot. I prithee be my god.

TRINCULO By this light, a most perfidious and drunken monster. When's god's asleep, he'll rob his bottle.

CALIBAN [*to Stephano:*] I'll kiss thy foot. I'll swear myself thy subject.

STEPHANO Come on then: down, and swear. [*Caliban kneels.*

TRINCULO I shall laugh myself to death at this puppy-headed monster: a most scurvy monster: I could find in my heart to beat him –

STEPHANO Come, kiss. [*Caliban kisses his foot.*

TRINCULO But that the poor monster's in drink. An abominable monster!

CALIBAN I'll show thee the best springs; I'll pluck thee berries;
I'll fish for thee, and get thee wood enough.
A plague upon the tyrant that I serve!
I'll bear him no more sticks, but follow thee,

Thou wondrous man.

TRINCULO A most ridiculous monster, to make a wonder of a poor drunkard!

CALIBAN I prithee, let me bring thee where crabs grow;
And I with my long nails will dig thee pig-nuts;
Show thee a jay's nest, and instruct thee how
To snare the nimble marmoset: I'll bring thee
To clustering filberts, and sometimes I'll get thee
Young scamels from the rock. Wilt thou go with me?

STEPHANO I prithee now, lead the way without any more talking – Trinculo, the King and all our company else being drowned, we will inherit here. [*To Caliban:*] Here; bear my bottle. – Fellow Trinculo, we'll fill him by and by again.

CALIBAN [*sings drunkenly:*] Farewell master; farewell, farewell.

TRINCULO A howling monster; a drunken monster.

CALIBAN [*sings:*] No more dams I'll make for fish,
Nor fetch in firing
At requiring,
Nor scrape trenchering, nor wash dish.
'Ban, 'Ban, Ca-Caliban
Has a new master. Get a new man!
Freedom, high-day! High-day, freedom! Freedom, high-day, freedom!

STEPHANO O brave monster; lead the way. [*Exeunt.*

ACT 3

Scene 1. *Before Prospero's cell.*

Enter FERDINAND, *bearing a log.*

FERDINAND There be some sports are painful, and their labour
Delight in them sets off; some kinds of baseness
Are nobly undergone; and most poor matters
Point to rich ends. This my mean task
Would be as heavy to me as odious, but
The mistress which I serve quickens what's dead,
And makes my labours pleasures. O, she is
Ten times more gentle than her father's crabbed;
And he's composed of harshness. I must remove
Some thousands of these logs, and pile them up,
Upon a sore injunction. My sweet mistress
Weeps when she sees me work, and says such baseness
Had never like executor. I forget;
But these sweet thoughts do even refresh my labours –
Most busil'est when I do it.

Enter MIRANDA, *followed by* PROSPERO *at a distance.*

MIRANDA Alas, now pray you,
Work not so hard. I would the lightning had
Burnt up those logs that you are enjoined to pile.
Pray set it down, and rest you. When this burns,
'Twill weep for having wearied you. My father
Is hard at study; pray now, rest yourself;
He's safe for these three hours.

FERDINAND O most dear mistress,
The sun will set before I shall discharge
What I must strive to do.

MIRANDA If you'll sit down,
I'll bear your logs the while: pray give me that;
I'll carry it to the pile.

FERDINAND No, precious creature,
I had rather crack my sinews, break my back,
Than you should such dishonour undergo
While I sit lazy by.

MIRANDA It would become me
As well as it does you; and I should do it
With much more ease: for my good will is to it,
And yours it is against.

PROSPERO [*aside:*] Poor worm, thou art infected,
This visitation shown it.

MIRANDA You look wearily.

FERDINAND No, noble mistress, 'tis fresh morning with me
When you are by at night. I do beseech you,
Chiefly that I might set it in my prayers,
What is your name?

MIRANDA Miranda. – O my father,
I have broke your hest to say so!

FERDINAND Admired Miranda!
Indeed the top of admiration, worth

What's dearest to the world! Full many a lady
I have eyed with best regard, and many a time
Th' harmony of their tongues hath into bondage
Brought my too diligent ear. For several virtues
Have I liked several women; never any
With so full soul, but some defect in her
Did quarrel with the noblest grace she owed,
And put it to the foil. But you, O you,
So perfect, and so peerless, are created
Of every creature's best.

MIRANDA I do not know
One of my sex; no woman's face remember,
Save, from my glass, mine own; nor have I seen
More that I may call men than you, good friend,
And my dear father. How features are abroad,
I am skilless of; but, by my modesty
(The jewel in my dower), I would not wish
Any companion in the world but you;
Nor can imagination form a shape,
Besides yourself, to like of. But I prattle
Something too wildly, and my father's precepts
I therein do forget.

FERDINAND I am, in my condition,
A prince, Miranda; I do think, a king –
I would not so! – and would no more endure
This wooden slavery, than to suffer
The flesh-fly blow my mouth. Hear my soul speak:
The very instant that I saw you, did
My heart fly to your service; there resides
To make me slave to it; and for your sake
Am I this patient log-man.

MIRANDA Do you love me?

FERDINAND O heaven, O earth, bear witness to this sound,
And crown what I profess with kind event
If I speak true; if hollowly, invert
What best is boded me to mischief! I,
Beyond all limit of what else i'th' world,
Do love, prize, honour you.

MIRANDA I am a fool
To weep at what I am glad of.

PROSPERO [*aside:*] Fair encounter
Of two most rare affections: heavens rain grace
On that which breeds between 'em!

FERDINAND Wherefore weep you?

MIRANDA At mine unworthiness, that dare not offer
What I desire to give, and much less take
What I shall die to want. But this is trifling;
And all the more it seeks to hide itself,
The bigger bulk it shows. Hence, bashful cunning,
And prompt me, pain and holy innocence.
I am your wife, if you will marry me;
If not, I'll die your maid: to be your fellow
You may deny me, but I'll be your servant,
Whether you will or no.

FERDINAND [*kneeling:*] My mistress, dearest;
And I thus humble ever.

MIRANDA My husband then?

FERDINAND Ay, with a heart as willing
As bondage e'er of freedom: here's my hand.

MIRANDA And mine, with my heart in't; and now farewell
Till half an hour hence.

FERDINAND A thousand thousand!

[*Exeunt Miranda and Ferdinand separately.*

PROSPERO So glad of this as they I cannot be,
Who are surprised with all; but my rejoicing
At nothing can be more. I'll to my book,
For yet, ere supper-time, must I perform
Much business appertaining.

[*Exit.*

Scene 2. *Another part of the island.*

Enter CALIBAN, STEPHANO *and* TRINCULO.

STEPHANO [*to Trinculo:*] Tell not me. When the butt is out we will drink water; not a drop before. Therefore bear up, and board 'em. [*To Caliban:*] Servant-monster, drink to me.

TRINCULO 'Servant-monster'? The folly of this island! They say there's but five upon this isle; we are three of them. If th'other two be brained like us, the state totters.

STEPHANO Drink, servant-monster, when I bid thee. Thy eyes are almost set in thy head.

TRINCULO Where should they be set else? He were a brave monster indeed, if they were set in his tail.

STEPHANO My man-monster hath drowned his tongue in sack; for my part, the sea cannot drown me. I swam, ere I could recover the shore, five-and-thirty leagues, off and on. By this light, thou shalt be my lieutenant, monster, or my standard.

TRINCULO Your lieutenant if you list; he's no standard.

STEPHANO We'll not run, Monsieur Monster.

TRINCULO Nor go neither; but you'll lie, like dogs, and yet say nothing neither.

STEPHANO Moon-calf, speak once in thy life, if thou beest a good moon-calf.

CALIBAN How does thy honour? Let me lick thy shoe.
I'll not serve him; he is not valiant.

TRINCULO Thou liest, most ignorant monster; I am in case to justle a constable. Why, thou debauched fish thou, was there ever a man a coward, that hath drunk so much sack as I today? Wilt thou tell a monstrous lie, being but half a fish, and half a monster?

CALIBAN Lo, how he mocks me! Wilt thou let him, my lord?

TRINCULO 'Lord', quoth he! That a monster should be such a natural!

CALIBAN Lo, lo, again! Bite him to death, I prithee.

STEPHANO Trinculo, keep a good tongue in your head: if you prove a mutineer, – the next tree! The poor monster's my subject, and he shall not suffer indignity.

CALIBAN I thank my noble lord. Wilt thou be pleased to hearken once again to the suit I made to thee?

STEPHANO Marry will I: kneel and repeat it. I will stand, and so shall Trinculo. [*Caliban kneels.*

Enter ARIEL, *invisible to them.*

CALIBAN As I told thee before, I am subject to a tyrant, a sorcerer, that by his cunning hath cheated me of the island.

ARIEL Thou liest.

CALIBAN [*to Trinculo:*] Thou liest, thou jesting monkey, thou!
I would my valiant master would destroy thee.
I do not lie.

STEPHANO Trinculo, if you trouble him any more in's tale, by this hand, I will supplant some of your teeth.

TRINCULO Why, I said nothing.

STEPHANO Mum, than, and no more. [*To Caliban:*] Proceed.

CALIBAN I say, by sorcery he got this isle;
From me he got it. If thy greatness will
Revenge it on him – for I know thou dar'st,
But this thing dare not –

STEPHANO That's most certain.

CALIBAN Thou shalt be lord of it, and I'll serve thee.

STEPHANO How now shall this be compassed? Canst thou bring me to the party?

CALIBAN Yea, yea, my lord. I'll yield him thee asleep,
Where thou mayst knock a nail into his head.

ARIEL Thou liest, thou canst not.

CALIBAN What a pied ninny's this! – Thou scurvy patch! –
I do beseech thy greatness, give him blows,
And take his bottle from him. When that's gone,
He shall drink nought but brine, for I'll not show him
Where the quick freshes are.

STEPHANO Trinculo, run into no further danger! Interrupt the monster one word further, and, by this hand, I'll turn my mercy out of doors, and make a stockfish of thee.

TRINCULO Why, what did I? I did nothing. I'll go further off.

STEPHANO Didst thou not say he lied?

ARIEL Thou liest.

STEPHANO Do I so? Take thou that. [*He strikes Trinculo.*] As you like this, give me the lie another time.

TRINCULO I did not give the lie. Out o' your wits, and hearing too? A pox o' your bottle! This can sack and drinking do. A murrain on your monster, and the devil take your fingers!

CALIBAN Ha, ha, ha!

STEPHANO Now, forward with your tale. [*To Trinculo:*] Prithee stand further off.

CALIBAN Beat him enough; after a little time,
I'll beat him too.

STEPHANO Stand further. – Come, proceed.

CALIBAN Why, as I told thee, 'tis a custom with him
I'th'afternoon to sleep: there thou mayst brain him,
Having first seized his books; or with a log
Batter his skull, or paunch him with a stake,
Or cut his wezand with thy knife. Remember
First to possess his books; for without them
He's but a sot, as I am; nor hath not
One spirit to command: they all do hate him
As rootedly as I. Burn but his books.
He has brave útensils (for so he calls them),
Which, when he has a house, he'll deck withal.
And that most deeply to consider is
The beauty of his daughter. He himself
Calls her a nonpareil: I never saw a woman
But only Sycorax (my dam) and she;
But she as far surpasseth Sycorax
As great'st does least.

STEPHANO Is it so brave a lass?

CALIBAN Ay lord, she will become thy bed, I warrant,
And bring thee forth brave brood.

STEPHANO Monster, I will kill this man; his daughter and I will be king and queen – save our graces! – and Trinculo and thyself shall be viceroys. Dost thou like the plot, Trinculo?

TRINCULO Excellent.

STEPHANO Give me thy hand. I am sorry I beat thee; but, while thou liv'st, keep a good tongue in thy head.

CALIBAN Within this half hour will he be asleep.
Wilt thou destroy him then?

STEPHANO Ay, on mine honour.

ARIEL [*aside:*] This will I tell my master.

CALIBAN Thou mak'st me merry: I am full of pleasure.
Let us be jocund. Will you troll the catch
You taught me but while-ere?

STEPHANO At thy request, monster, I will do reason, any reason. – Come on, Trinculo, let us sing.

STEPHANO *and* TRINCULO *sing:*

Flout'em, and scout 'em,
And scout'em, and flout 'em:
Thought is free.

CALIBAN That's not the tune.

ARIEL *plays the tune on a tabor and pipe.*

STEPHANO What is this same?

TRINCULO This is the tune of our catch, played by the picture of Nobody.

STEPHANO [*towards Ariel:*] If thou beest a man, show thyself in thy likeness; if thou beest a devil, take't as thou list.

TRINCULO O forgive me my sins!

STEPHANO He that dies, pays all debts: I defy thee. Mercy upon us!

CALIBAN Art thou afeard?

STEPHANO No, monster, not I.

CALIBAN Be not afeard. The isle is full of noises,
Sounds and sweet airs, that give delight, and hurt not:
Sometimes a thousand twangling instruments
Will hum about mine ears; and sometime voices,
That, if I then had waked after long sleep,
Will make me sleep again; and then, in dreaming,
The clouds methought would open, and show riches
Ready to drop upon me, that when I waked,

I cried to dream again.

STEPHANO This will prove a brave kingdom to me, where I shall have my music for nothing.

CALIBAN When Prospero is destroyed.

STEPHANO That shall be by and by: I remember the story.

[*Exit Ariel, playing.*

TRINCULO The sound is going away. Let's follow it, and after do our work.

STEPHANO Lead, monster, we'll follow. I would I could see this taborer: he lays it on.

TRINCULO [*to Caliban:*] Wilt come? I'll follow Stephano.

[*Exeunt.*

Scene 3. *Another part of the island.*

Enter ALONSO, SEBASTIAN, ANTONIO, GONZALO, ADRIAN *and* FRANCISCO.

GONZALO By'r lakin, I can go no further, sir.
My old bones ache. Here's a maze trod, indeed,
Through forthrights and meanders. By your patience,
I needs must rest me.

ALONSO Old lord, I cannot blame thee,
Who am myself attached with weariness,
To th' dulling of my spirits. Sit down, and rest.
Even here I will put off my hope, and keep it
No longer for my flatterer. He is drowned
Whom thus we stray to find, and the sea mocks
Our frústrate search on land. Well, let him go.

ANTONIO [*aside to Sebastian:*]
I am right glad that he's so out of hope.
Do not, for one repulse, forgo the purpose

That you resolved t'effect.

SEBASTIAN [*aside to Antonio:*] The next advantage
Will we take throughly.

ANTONIO Let it be tonight,
For, now they are oppressed with travail, they
Will not, nor cannot, use such vigilance
As when they are fresh.

SEBASTIAN I say, tonight. No more.

Solemn and strange music; and PROSPER *on the top (invisible).*

ALONSO What harmony is this? My good friends, hark!

GONZALO Marvellous sweet music!

Enter several strange SHAPES, *bringing in a banquet; and dance about it with gentle actions of salutations; and, inviting the King, &c. to eat, they depart.*

ALONSO Give us kind keepers, heavens! What were these?

SEBASTIAN A living drollery. Now I will believe
That there are unicorns; that in Arabian
There is one tree, the phoenix' throne, one phoenix
At this hour reigning there.

ANTONIO I'll believe both;
And what does else want credit, come to me,
And I'll be sworn 'tis true. Travellers ne'er did lie,
Though fools at home condemn 'em.

GONZALO If in Naples
I should report this now, would they believe me
If I should say I saw such islanders? –
For, certes, these are people of the island,
Who, though they are of monstrous shape, yet note
Their manners are more gentle-kind than of
Our human generation you shall find

Many, nay, almost any.

PROSPERO [*aside:*] Honest lord,
Thou hast said well: for some of you there present
Are worse than devils.

ALONSO I cannot too much muse;
Such shapes, such gesture, and such sound, expressing
(Although they want the use of tongue) a kind
Of excellent dumb discourse.

PROSPERO [*aside:*] Praise in departing.

FRANCISCO They vanished strangely.

SEBASTIAN No matter, since
They have left their viands behind; for we have stomachs.
Will't please you taste of what is here?

ALONSO Not I.

GONZALO Faith, sir, you need not fear. When we were boys,
Who would believe that there were mountaineers
Dewlapped like bulls, whose throats had hanging at 'em
Wallets of flesh? Or that there were such men
Whose heads stood in their breasts? Which now we find
Each putter-out of five for one will bring us
Good warrant of.

ALONSO I will stand to, and feed,
Although my last; no matter, since I feel
The best is past. Brother, my lord the Duke,
Stand to and do as we.

Thunder and lightning. Enter ARIEL *like a harpy, claps his wings upon the table, and, with a quaint device, the banquet vanishes.*

ARIEL You are three men of sin, whom destiny –
That hath to instrument this lower world
And what is in't – the never-surfeited sea
Hath caused to belch up you, and on this island
Where man doth not inhabit, you 'mongst men
Being most unfit to live. I have made you mad;
And even with suchlike valour, men hang and drown
Their proper selves. [*Several men draw their swords:*]
You fools! I and my fellows
Are ministers of Fate. The elements
Of whom your swords are tempered may as well
Wound the loud winds, or with bemocked-at stabs
Kill the still-closing waters, as diminish
One dowl that's in my plume; my fellow-ministers
Are like invulnerable. If you could hurt,
Your swords are now too massy for your strengths,
And will not be uplifted. But remember
(For that's my business to you) that you three
From Millaine did supplant good Prospero;
Exposed unto the sea (which hath requite it)
Him and his innocent child; for which foul deed,
The powers, delaying, not forgetting, have
Incensed the seas and shores, yea, all the creatures,
Against your peace. Thee of thy son, Alonso,
They have bereft; and do pronounce by me,
Ling'ring perdition (worse than any death
Can be at once) shall step by step attend
You and your ways; whose wraths to guard
you from –
Which here, in this most desolate isle, else falls
Upon your heads – is nothing but heart's sorrow,
And a clear life ensuing.

He vanishes in thunder. Then, to soft music,
enter the SHAPES *again, and dance with mocks*
and mows; and depart, carrying out the table.

PROSPERO [*aside:*] Bravely the figure of this harpy hast thou
Performed, my Ariel; a grace it had, devouring;
Of my instruction hast thou nothing bated
In what thou hadst to say. So, with good life
And observation strange, my meaner ministers
Their several kinds have done. My high charms work,
And these, mine enemies, are all knit up
In their distractions: they now are in my power;
And in these fits I leave them, whilst I visit
Young Ferdinand (whom they suppose is drowned)
And his and mine loved darling. [*Exit above.*

GONZALO I'th' name of something holy, sir, why stand you
In this strange stare?

ALONSO O, it is monstrous, monstrous!
Methought the billows spoke, and told me of it;
The winds did sing it to me; and the thunder,
That deep and dreadful organ-pipe, pronounced
The name of Prosper: it did bass my trespass.
Therefore my son i'th'ooze is bedded; and
I'll seek him deeper than e'er plummet sounded,
And with him there lie mudded. [*Exit.*

SEBASTIAN But one fiend at a time,
I'll fight their legions o'er.

ANTONIO I'll be thy second. [*Exeunt.*

GONZALO All three of them are desperate: their great guilt,
Like poison given to work a great time after,
Now 'gins to bite the spirits. I do beseech you,
That are of suppler joints, follow them swiftly,

And hinder them from what this ecstasy
May now provoke them to.

ADRIAN [*to Francisco:*] Follow, I pray you.

[*Exeunt.*

ACT 4

Scene 1. *Before Prospero's cell.*

Enter PROSPERO, FERDINAND *and* MIRANDA.

PROSPERO [*to Ferdinand:*] If I have too austerely punished you,
Your compensation makes amends, for I
Have given you here a third of mine own life,
Or that for which I live: who once again
I tender to thy hand. All thy vexations
Were but my trials of thy love, and thou
Hast strangely stood the test. Here, afore Heaven,
I ratify this my rich gift: O Ferdinand,
Do not smile at me that I boast of her,
For thou shalt find she will outstrip all praise
And make it halt behind her.

FERDINAND I do believe it
Against an oracle.

PROSPERO Then, as my gift, and thine own acquisition
Worthily purchased, take my daughter. But
If thou dost break her virgin-knot before
All sanctimonious ceremonies may

With full and holy rite be ministered,
No sweet aspersion shall the heavens let fall
To make this contract grow; but barren hate,
Sour-eyed disdain, and discord shall bestrew
The union of your bed with weeds so loathly
That you shall hate it both. Therefore take heed,
As Hymen's lamp shall light you.

FERDINAND As I hope
For quiet days, fair issue, and long life,
With such love as 'tis now: the murkiest den,
The most oppórtune place, the strong'st suggestion
Our worser genius can, shall never melt
Mine honour into lust, to take away
The edge of that day's celebration,
When I shall think, or Phoebus' steeds are foundered,
Or Night kept chained below.

PROSPERO Fairly spoke.
Sit, then, and talk with her: she is thine own. –
What, Ariel; my industrious servant Ariel!

Enter ARIEL.

ARIEL What would my potent master? Here I am.

PROSPERO Thou and thy meaner fellows your last service
Did worthily perform, and I must use you
In such another trick. Go bring the rabble
(O'er whom I give thee power) here to this place.
Incite them to quick motion, for I must
Bestow upon the eyes of this young couple
Some vanity of mine art: it is my promise,
And they expect it from me.

ARIEL Presently?

PROSPERO Ay, with a twink.

ARIEL Before you can say 'come' and 'go',
And breathe twice, and cry 'so, so',
Each one, tripping on his toe,
Will be here with mop and mow.
Do you love me, master? No?

PROSPERO Dearly, my delicate Ariel. Do not approach
Till thou dost hear me call.

ARIEL Well; I conceive. [*Exit.*

PROSPERO [*to Ferdinand:*]
Look thou be true. Do not give dalliance
Too much the rein: the strongest oaths are straw
To th' fire i'th' blood. Be more abstemious,
Or else good night your vow.

FERDINAND I warrant you, sir,
The white cold virgin snow upon my heart
Abates the ardour of my liver.

PROSPERO Well. –
Now come, my Ariel. Bring a corollary,
Rather than want a spirit; appear, and pertly! –
No tongue! All eyes! Be silent! [*Soft music.*

Enter IRIS.

IRIS Ceres, most bounteous lady: thy rich leas
Of wheat, rye, barley, vetches, oats, and peace;
Thy turfy mountains, where live nibbling sheep,
And flat meads thatched with stover, them to keep;
Thy banks with pionèd and twillèd brims,
Which spongy April at thy hest betrims
To make cold nymphs chaste crowns; and thy broom-groves,
Whose shadow the dismissèd bachelor loves,
Being lass-lorn; thy pole-clipped vineyard,

And thy sea-marge, sterile and rocky-hard,
Where thou thyself dost air: the Queen o'th' Sky,
Whose wat'ry arch and messenger am I,
Bids thee leave these, and with her sovereign grace,

A peacock-drawn chariot, bearing JUNO, *descends.*

Here on this grass-plot, in this very place,
To come and sport; her peacocks fly amain.
Approach, rich Ceres, her to entertain.

Enter CERES.

CERES [*to Iris:*] Hail, many-coloured messenger, that ne'er
Dost disobey the wife of Jupiter;
Who, with thy saffron wings, upon my flowers
Diffusest honey-drops, refreshing showers,
And with each end of thy blue bow dost crown
My bosky acres and my unshrubbed down,
Rich scarf to my proud earth: why hath thy queen
Summoned me hither, to this short-grassed green?

IRIS A contract of true love to celebrate,
And some donation freely to estate
On the blessed lovers.

CERES Tell me, heavenly bow,
If Venus or her son, as thou dost know,
Do now attend the Queen. Since they did plot
The means that dusky Dis my daughter got,
Her and her blind boy's scandalled company
I have forsworn.

IRIS Of her society
Be not afraid. I met her deity
Cutting the clouds towards Paphos, and her son
Dove-drawn with her: here thought they to have done

Some wanton charm upon this man and maid
(Whose vows are, that no bed-rite shall be paid
Till Hymen's torch be lighted); but in vain.
Mars's hot minion is returned again;
Her waspish-headed son has broke his arrows,
Swears he will shoot no more, but play with sparrows
And be a boy right out.

JUNO *alights from her chariot.*

CERES Highest Queen of state,
Great Juno comes; I know her by her gait.

JUNO How does my bounteous sister? Go with me
To bless this twain, that they may prosperous be,
And honoured in their issue.

JUNO *and* CERES *sing together:*

Honour, riches, marriage-blessing,
Long continuance, and increasing,
Hourly joys be still upon you!
Juno sings her blessings on you.
Earth's increase, foison plenty,
Barns and garners never empty,
Vines with clust'ring bunches growing,
Plants with goodly burden bowing;
Spring come to you, at the farthest,
In the very end of harvest!
Scarcity and want shall shun you;
Ceres' blessing so is on you.

FERDINAND This is a most majestic vision, and
Harmonious charmingly: may I be bold
To think these spirits?

PROSPERO Spirits, which by mine art

I have from their confines called to enact
My present fancies.

FERDINAND Let me live here ever;
So rare a wondered father and a wise
Make this place Paradise.

[Juno and Ceres whisper, and send Iris on employement.

PROSPERO Sweet now, silence:
Juno and Ceres whisper seriously:
There's something else to do. Hush, and be mute,
Or else our spell is marred.

IRIS You nymphs, called Naiads, of the windring brooks,
With your sedged crowns and ever harmless looks,
Leave your crisp channels, and on this green land
Answer your summons; Juno does command.
Come, temperate nymphs, and help to celebrate
A contract of true love: be not too late.

Enter some NYMPHS.

You sunburnt sicklemen, of August weary,
Come hither from the furrow, and be merry.
Make holiday: your rye-straw hats put on,
And these fresh nymphs encounter every one
In country footing.

Enter certain REAPERS, *properly habited. They join with the Nymphs in a graceful dance; towards the end whereof, Prospero starts suddenly, and speaks.*

PROSPERO [*aside:*] I had forgot that foul conspiracy
Of the beast Caliban and his confederates
Against my life: the minute of their plot
Is almost come. [*To the spirits:*] Well done! Avoid:
no more.

Juno and Ceres ascend in the chariot. To a strange, hollow and confused noise, the other spirits gloomily vanish.

FERDINAND This is strange: your father's in some passion
That works him strongly.

MIRANDA Never till this day
Saw I him touched with anger so distempered.

PROSPERO You do look, my son, in a moved sort,
As if you were dismayed: be cheerful, sir.
Our revels now are ended. These our actors
(As I foretold you) were all spirits, and
Are melted into air, into thin air;
And, like the baseless fabric of this vision,
The cloud-capped towers, the gorgeous palaces,
The solemn temples, the great globe itself,
Yea, all which it inherit, shall dissolve,
And, like this insubstantial pageant faded,
Leave not a rack behind. We are such stuff
As dreams are made on; and our little life
Is rounded with a sleep. Sir, I am vexed.
Bear with my weakness; my old brain is troubled;
Be not disturbed with my infirmity.
If you be pleased, retire into my cell,
And there repose. A turn or two I'll walk,
To still my beating mind.

FERDINAND, MIRANDA We wish your peace.
[*Exeunt Ferdinand and Miranda.*

PROSPERO Come with a thought! I thank thee, Ariel: come!

Enter ARIEL.

ARIEL Thy thoughts I cleave to. What's thy pleasure?

PROSPERO Spirit,
We must prepare to meet with Caliban.

ARIEL Ay, my commander; when I presented Ceres,
I thought to have told thee of it, but I feared
Lest I might anger thee.

PROSPERO Say again, where didst thou leave these varlets?

ARIEL I told you, sir, they were red-hot with drinking;
So full of valour, that they smote the air
For breathing in their faces, beat the ground
For kissing of their feet; yet always bending
Towards their project. Then I beat my tabor,
At which, like unbacked colts, they pricked their ears,
Advanced their eyelids, lifted up their noses
As they smelt music. So I charmed their ears
That, calf-like, they my lowing followed, through
Toothed briers, sharp furzes, pricking gorse,
and thorns,
Which entered their frail shins. At last I left them
I'th' filthy mantled pool beyond your cell,
There dancing up to th' chins, that the foul lake
O'er-stunk their feet.

PROSPERO This was well done, my bird.
Thy shape invisible retain thou still.
The trumpery in my house, go, brig it hither,
For stale to catch these thieves.

ARIEL I go, I go. [*Exit.*

PROSPERO A devil, a born devil, on whose nature
Nurture can never stick; on whom my pains,
Humanely taken, all, all lost, quite lost;
And as with age his body uglier grows,
So his mind cankers. I will plague them all,
Even to roaring.

Enter ARIEL, *laden with glistering apparel, &c.*

Come, hang them on this line.

Prospero and Ariel remain, invisible to others.
Enter CALIBAN, STEPHANO *and* TRINCULO, *all wet.*

CALIBAN Pray you, tread softly, that the blind mole may
Not hear a footfall: we now are near his cell.

STEPHANO Monster, your fairy, which you say is a harmless fairy, has done little better than played the Jack with us.

TRINCULO Monster, I do smell all horse-piss, at which my nose is in great indignation.

STEPHANO So is mine. Do you hear, monster? If I should take a displeasure against you, look you –

TRINCULO Thou wert but a lost monster.

CALIBAN Good my lord, give me thy favour still.
Be patient, for the prize I'll bring thee to
Shall hoodwink this mischance: therefore, speak softly;
All's hushed as midnight yet.

TRINCULO Ay, but to lose our bottles in the pool!

STEPHANO There is not only disgrace and dishonour in that, monster, but an infinite loss.

TRINCULO That's more to me than my wetting; yet this is your harmless fairy, monster.

STEPHANO I will fetch off my bottle, though I be o'er ears for my labour.

CALIBAN Prithee, my king, be quiet. Seest thou here:
This is the mouth o'th' cell. No noise, and enter.
Do that good mischief which may make this island
Thine own for ever, and I, thy Caliban,
For aye thy foot-licker.

STEPHANO Give me thy hand. I do begin to have bloody thoughts.

TRINCULO O King Stephano, O peer! O worthy Stephano, look what a wardrobe here is for thee!

CALIBAN Let it alone, thou fool: it is but trash.

TRINCULO O, ho, monster! We know what belongs to a frippery. [*He tries on a gown.*] O King Stephano!

STEPHANO Put off that gown, Trinculo. By this hand, I'll have that gown.

TRINCULO Thy grace shall have it.

CALIBAN The dropsy drown this fool! What do you mean,
To dote thus on such luggage? Let's alone,
And do the murder first. If he awake,
From teo to crown he'll fill our skins with pinches,
Make us strange stuff.

STEPHANO Be you quiet, monster. – Mistress line, is not this my jerkin? Now is the jerkin under the line: now, jerkin, you are like to lose your hair, and prove a bald jerkin.

TRINCULO Do, do! We steal by line and level, an't like your grace.

STEPHANO I thank thee for that jest; here's garment for't. Wit shall not go unrewarded while I am king of this country. 'Steal by line and level' is an excellent pass of pate; there's another garment for't.

TRINCULO Monster, come, put some lime upon your fingers, and away with the rest.

CALIBAN I will have none on't: we shall lose our time,
And all be turned to barnacles, or to apes
With foreheads villainous low.

STEPHANO Monster, lay-to your fingers: help to bear this away where my hogshead of wine is, or I'll turn you out of my kingdom. Go to, carry this.

TRINCULO And this.

STEPHANO Ay, and this.

They load Caliban with garments. A noise of hunters heard. Enter divers SPIRITS, *in shape of dogs and hounds, hunting the trio; Prospero and Ariel setting them on.*

PROSPERO Hey, Mountain, hey!

ARIEL Silver: there it goes, Silver!

PROSPERO Fury, Fury! There, Tyrant, there! Hark, hark!

[*Exeunt Caliban, Stephano and Trinculo, pursued.*

Go, charge my goblins that they grind their joints
With dry convulsions, shorten up their sinews
With agèd cramps, and more pinch-spotted make them
Than pard or cat o' mountain. [*Yells within.*

ARIEL Hark, they roar.

PROSPERO Let them be hunted soundly. At this hour
Lies at my mercy all mine enemies.
Shortly shall all my labours end, and thou
Shalt have the air at freedom. For a little,
Follow, and do me service.

[*Exeunt.*

ACT 5

Scene 1. *Before Prospero's cell.*

Enter PROSPERO, *in his magic robes, and* ARIEL.

PROSPERO Now does my project gather to a head:
My charms crack not, my spirits obey, and Time
Goes upright with his carriage. How's the day?

ARIEL On the sixth hour, at which time, my lord,
You said our work should cease.

PROSPERO I did say so
When first I raised the tempest. Say, my spirit,
How fares the King and's followers?

ARIEL Confined together
In the same fashion as you gave in charge,
Just as you left them: all prisoners, sir,
In the line-grove which weather-fends your cell:
They cannot budge till your release. The King,
His brother, and yours, abide all three distracted,
And the remainder mourning over them,
Brimful of sorrow and dismay; but chiefly
Him you termed, sir, 'the good old lord, Gonzalo'.

His tears run down his beard like winter's drops
From eaves of reeds. Your charm so strongly
works 'em
That, if you now beheld them, your affections
Would become tender.

PROSPERO Dost thou think so, spirit?

ARIEL Mine would, sir, were I human.

PROSPERO And mine shall.
Hast thou (which art but air) a touch, a feeling
Of their afflictions, and shall not myself,
One of their kind, that relish all as sharply
Passion as they, be kindlier moved than thou art?
Though with their high wrongs I am struck to
th' quick,
Yet, with my nobler reason, 'gainst my fury
Do I take part: the rarer action is
In virtue than in vengeance: they being penitent,
The sole drift of my purpose doth extend
Not a frown further. Go, release them, Ariel.
My charms I'll break, their senses I'll restore,
And they shall be themselves.

ARIEL I'll fetch them, sir. [*Exit.*

Prospero draws a large horizontal circle with his staff.

PROSPERO Ye elves of hills, brooks, standing lakes and groves,
And ye, that on the sands with printless foot
Do chase the ebbing Neptune, and do fly him
When he comes back; you demi-puppets that
By moonshine do the green sour ringlets make,
Whereof the ewe not bites; and you, whose pastime
Is to make midnight mushrumps, that rejoice
To hear the solemn curfew; by whose aid

(Weak masters though ye be) I have bedimmed
The noontide sun, called forth the mutinous winds,
And 'twixt the green sea and the azured vault
Set roaring war: to the dread rattling thunder
Have I given fire, and rifted Jove's stout oak
With his own bolt; the strong-based promontory
Have I made shake, and by the spurs plucked up
The pine and cedar; graves at my command
Have waked their sleepers, oped, and let 'em forth
By my so potent art. But this rough magic
I here abjure; and when I have required
Some heavenly music (which even now I do)
To work mine end upon their senses that
This airy charm is for, I'll break my staff,
Bury it certain fathoms in the earth,
And deeper than did ever plummet sound
I'll drown my book. [*Solemn music.*

Here enters ARIEL *before; then* ALONSO, *with a frantic gesture, attended by* GONZALO; SEBASTIAN *and* ANTONIO *in like manner, attended by* ADRIAN *and* FRANCISCO: *they all enter the circle which Prospero had made, and there stand charmed; which Prospero observing, speaks.*

[*To Alonso:*] A solemn air, and the best comforter
To an unsettled fancy, cure thy brains
(Now useless), boiled within thy skull.
[*To Sebastian and Antonio:*] There stand,
For you are spell-stopped. –
Holy Gonzalo, honourable man,
Mine eyes, ev'n sociable to the show of thine,
Fall fellowly drops. [*Aside:*] The charm dissolves apace;
And as the morning steals upon the night,

Melting the darkness, so their rising senses
Begin to chase the ignorant fumes that mantle
Their clearer reason. – O good Gonzalo,
My true preserver, and a loyal sir
To him thou follow'st: I will pay thy graces
Home, both in word and deed. – Most cruelly
Didst thou, Alonso, use me and my daughter.
Thy brother was a furtherer in the act; –
Thou art pinched for't now, Sebastian.
[*To Antonio:*] Flesh and blood,
You, brother mine, that entertained ambition,
Expelled remorse and nature; who, with Sebastian
(Whose inward pinches therefore are most strong),
Would here have killed your king: I do forgive thee,
Unnatural though thou art. [*Aside:*] Their understanding
Begins to swell, and the approaching tide
Will shortly fill the reasonable shore
That now lies foul and muddy. Not one of them
That yet looks on me, or would know me. – Ariel,
Fetch me the hat and rapier in my cell. [*Exit Ariel.*
I will discase me, and myself present
As I was sometime Millaine. Quickly, spirit!
Thou shalt ere long be free.

Returning, ARIEL *sings, and helps to attire him.*

ARIEL Where the bee sucks, there suck I:
In a cowslip's bell I lie;
There I couch, when owls do cry.
On the bat's back I do fly
After summer merrily.
Merrily, merrily, shall I live now,

Under the blossom that hangs on the bough.

PROSPERO Why, that's my dainty Ariel! I shall miss thee,
But yet thou shalt have freedom. – So, so, so. –
To the King's ship, invisible as thou art;
There shalt thou find the mariners asleep
Under the hatches. The master and the boatswain
Being awake, enforce them to this place;
And presently, I prithee.

ARIEL I drink the air before me, and return
Or ere your pulse twice beat. [*Exit.*

GONZALO All torment, trouble, wonder and amazement
Inhabits here: some heavenly power guide us
Out of this fearful country!

PROSPERO Behold, sir King,
The wrongèd Duke of Millaine, Prospero:
For more assurance that a living prince
Does now speak to thee, I embrace thy body,
And to thee and thy company I bid
A hearty welcome.

ALONSO Whe'er thou be'st he or no,
Or some enchanted trifle to abuse me,
As late I have been, I not know. Thy pulse
Beats, as of flesh and blood; and, since I saw thee,
Th'affliction of my mind amends, with which
I fear a madness held me. This must crave –
And if this be at all – a most strange story.
Thy dukedom I resign, and do entreat
Thou pardon me my wrongs. But how should Prospero
Be living, and be here?

PROSPERO [*to Gonzalo:*] First, noble friend,
Let me embrace thine age, whose honour cannot

Be measured or confined.

GONZALO Whether this be,
Or be not, I'll not swear.

PROSPERO You do yet taste
Some subtleties o'th'isle, that will not let you
Believe things certain. – Welcome, my friends all!
[*Aside to Sebastian and Antonio:*]
But you, my brace of lords: were I so minded,
I here could pluck his Highness' frown upon you,
And justify you traitors. At this time
I will tell no tales.

SEBASTIAN [*aside:*] The devil speaks in him.

PROSPERO No. –
For you (most wicked sir), whom to call brother
Would even infect my mouth, I do forgive
Thy rankest fault – all of them; and require
My dukedom of thee, which perforce, I know,
Thou must restore.

ALONSO If thou beest Prospero,
Give us particulars of thy preservation,
How thou hast met us here, who three hours since
Were wracked upon this shore; where I have lost
(How sharp the point of this remembrance is!)
My dear son Ferdinand.

PROSPERO I am woe for't, sir.

ALONSO Irreparable is the loss, and patience
Says it is past her cure.

PROSPERO I rather think
You have not sought her help, of whose soft grace
For the like loss I have her sovereign aid,
And rest myself content.

ALONSO You the like loss?

PROSPERO As great to me as late; and, supportable
To make the dear loss, have I means much weaker
Than you may call to comfort you; for I
Have lost my daughter.

ALONSO A daughter?
O heavens, that they were living both in Naples,
The king and queen there! That they were, I wish
Myself were mudded in that oozy bed
Where my son lies. When did you lose your daughter?

PROSPERO In this last tempest. I perceive these lords
At this encounter do so much admire,
That they devour their reason, and scarce think
Their eyes do offices of truth, their words
Are natural breath. But, howsoe'er you have
Been justled from your senses, know for certain
That I am Prospero and that very Duke
Which was thrust forth of Millaine, who most strangely
Upon this shore (where you were wracked) was landed,
To be the lord on't. No more yet of this,
For 'tis a chronicle of day by day,
Not a relation for a breakfast, nor
Befitting this first meeting. Welcome, sir.
This cell's my court: here have I few attendants,
And subjects none abroad. Pray you, look in.
My dukedom since you have given me again,
I will requite you with as good a thing:
At least, bring forth a wonder, to content ye
As much as me my dukedom.

Here Prospero discovers FERDINAND *and* MIRANDA, *playing at chess.*

MIRANDA Sweet lord, you play me false.
FERDINAND My dearest love,
I would not for the world.
MIRANDA Yes, for a score of kingdoms you should wrangle,
And I would call it fair play.
ALONSO If this prove
A vision of the island, one dear son
Shall I twice lose.
SEBASTIAN A most high miracle!
FERDINAND [*emerging:*] Though the seas threaten, they are merciful;
I have cursed them without cause. [*He kneels.*
ALONSO Now all the blessings
Of a glad father compass thee about!
Arise, and say how thou cam'st here. [*Ferdinand rises.*
MIRANDA O wonder!
How many goodly creatures are there here!
How beauteous mankind is! O brave new world,
That has such people in't!
PROSPERO 'Tis new to thee.
ALONSO What is this maid, with whom thou wast at play?
Your eld'st acquaintance cannot be three hours.
Is she the goddess that hath severed us,
And brought us thus together?
FERDINAND Sir, she is mortal;
But, by immortal Providence, she's mine.
I chose her when I could not ask my father
For his advice, nor thought I had one. She
Is daughter to this famous Duke of Millaine,
Of whom so often I have heard renown,
But never saw before; of whom I have
Received a second life; and second father
This lady makes him to me.

ALONSO I am hers.
But O, how oddly will it sound, that I
Must ask my child forgiveness!

PROSPERO There, sir, stop.
Let us not burden our remembrance with
A heaviness that's gone.

GONZALO I have inly wept,
Or should have spoke ere this. Look down, you gods,
And on this couple drop a blessèd crown;
For it is you that have chalked forth the way
Which brought us hither.

ALONSO I say 'Amen', Gonzalo.

GONZALO Was Millaine thrust from Millaine, that his issue
Should become kings of Naples? O, rejoice
Beyond a common joy; and set it down
With gold on lasting pillars: in one voyage
Did Claribel her husband find at Tunis,
And Ferdinand, her brother, found a wife
Where he himself was lost, Prospero his dukedom
In a poor isle, and all of us ourselves
When no man was his own.

ALONSO [*to Ferdinand and Miranda:*] Give me your hands.
Let grief and sorrow still embrace his heart
That doth not wish you joy.

GONZALO Be it so. Amen.

Enter ARIEL, *with the* MASTER *and* BOATSWAIN *amazedly following.*

O look sir, look sir, here is more of us!
I prophesied, if a gallows were on land,
This fellow could not drown. [*To the Boatswain:*]
Now, Blasphemy,
That swear'st grace o'erboard: not an oath on shore?

Has thou no mouth by land? What is the news?

BOATSWAIN The best news is that we have safely found
Our king and company. The next, our ship,
Which but three glasses since we gave out split,
Is tight and yare and bravely rigged as when
We first put out to sea.

ARIEL [*aside to Prospero:*] Sir, all this service.
Have I done since I went.

PROSPERO [*aside to Ariel:*] My tricksy spirit!

ALONSO These are not natural events; they strengthen
From strange to stranger. Say, how came you hither?

BOATSWAIN If I did think, sir, I were well awake,
I'd strive to tell you. We were dead of sleep,
And (how, we know not) all clapped under hatches,
Where, but even now, with strange and several noises
Of roaring, shrieking, howling, jingling chains,
And mo diversity of sounds, all horrible,
We were awaked; straightway at liberty;
Where we, in all our trim, freshly beheld
Our royal, good, and gallant ship; our master
Cap'ring to eye her. On a trice, so please you,
Even in a dream, were we divided from them,
And were brought moping hither.

ARIEL [*aside to Prospero:*] Was't well done?

PROSPERO [*aside to him:*] Bravely, my diligence; thou shalt be free.

ALONSO This is as strange a maze as e'er men trod.
And there is in this business more than nature
Was ever conduct of. Some oracle
Must rectify our knowledge.

PROSPERO Sir, my liege,
Do not infest your mind with beating on
The strangeness of this business. At picked leisure

(Which shall be shortly single), I'll resolve you,
Which to you shall seem probable, of every
These happened accidents. Till when, be cheerful
And think of each thing well. [*Aside to Ariel:*]
Come hither, spirit.
Set Caliban and his companions free:
Untie the spell. [*Exit Ariel.*
[*To Alonso:*] How fares my gracious sir?
There are yet missing of your company
Some few odd lads that you remember not.

Enter ARIEL, *driving in* CALIBAN, STEPHANO *and* TRINCULO *in their stolen apparel.*

STEPHANO Every man shift for all the rest, and let no man take care for himself; for all is but fortune. Coragio, bully-monster, coragio!

TRINCULO If these be true spies which I wear in my head, here's a goodly sight.

CALIBAN O Setebos, these be brave spirits indeed!
How fine my master is! I am afraid
He will chastise me.

SEBASTIAN Ha, ha!
What things are these, my lord Autonio?
Will money buy 'em?

ANTONIO Very like: one of them
Is a plain fish, and no doubt marketable.

PROSPERO Mark but the badges of these men, my lords,
Then say if they be true. This mis-shapen knave:
His mother was a witch, and one so strong
That could control the moon, make flows and ebbs,
And deal in her command without her power.
These three have robbed me, and this demi-devil

(For he's a bastard one) had plotted with them
To take my life. Two of these fellows you
Must know and own; this thing of darkness I
Acknowledge mine.

CALIBAN I shall be pinched to death.

ALONSO Is not this Stephano, my drunken butler?

SEBASTIAN He is drunk now; where had he wine?

ALONSO And Trinculo is reeling-ripe: where should they
Find this grand liquor that hath gilded 'em?
[*To Trinculo:*] How cam'st thou in this pickle?

TRINCULO I have been in such a pickle since I saw you last that, I fear me, will never out of my bones: I shall not fear fly-blowing.

SEBASTIAN Why, how now, Stephano?

STEPHANO O touch me not: I am not Stephano, but a cramp.

PROSPERO You'd be king o'th'isle, sirrah?

STEPHANO I should have been a sore one then.

ALONSO [*indicating Caliban:*]
This is a strange thing as e'er I looked on.

PROSPERO He is as disproportioned in his manners
As in his shape. [*To Caliban:*] Go, sirrah, to my cell;
Take with you your companions; as you look
To have my pardon, trim it handsomely.

CALIBAN Ay, that I will; and I'll be wise hereafter,
And seek for grace. What a thrice-double ass
Was I, to take this drunkard for a god,
And worship this dull fool!

PROSPERO Go to, away.

ALONSO [*to Stephano and Trinculo:*]
Hence, and bestow your luggage where you found it.

SEBASTIAN Or stole it rather.

[*Exeunt Caliban, Stephano and Trinculo.*

PROSPERO [*to Alonso:*] Sir, I invite your Highness and your train
To my poor cell, where you shall take your rest
For this one night; which, part of it, I'll waste
With such discourse as, I not doubt, shall make it
Go quick away: the story of my life,
And the particular accidents gone by
Since I came to this isle. And in the morn
I'll bring you to your ship, and so to Naples,
Where I have hope to see the nuptial
Of these our dear-belov'd solemnizèd;
And thence retire me to my Millaine, where
Every third thought shall be my grave.

ALONSO I long
To hear the story of your life, which must
Take the ear strangely.

PROSPERO I'll deliver all;
And promise you calm seas, auspicious gales,
And sail so expeditious that shall catch
Your royal fleet far off. – My Ariel, chick,
That is thy charge; then to the elements
Be free, and fare thou well. [*Exit Ariel.*
– Please you, draw near.
[*Exeunt all but Prospero.*

EPILOGUE

spoken by PROSPERO.

Now my charms are all o'erthrown,
And what strength I have's mine own,
Which is most faint. Now, 'tis true,
I must be here confined by you,
Or sent to Naples. Let me not,
Since I have my dukedom got,
And pardoned the deceiver, dwell
In this bare island, by your spell;
But release me from my bands,
With the help of your good hands.
Gentle breath of yours my sails
Must fill, or else my project fails,
Which was to please. Now I want
Spirits to enforce, art to enchant;
And my ending is despair,
Unless I be relieved by prayer
Which pierces so, that it assaults
Mercy itself, and frees all faults.
As you from crimes would pardoned be,
Let your indulgence set me free.

[*Exit.*

FINIS.

INTERNATIONAL BESTSELLER

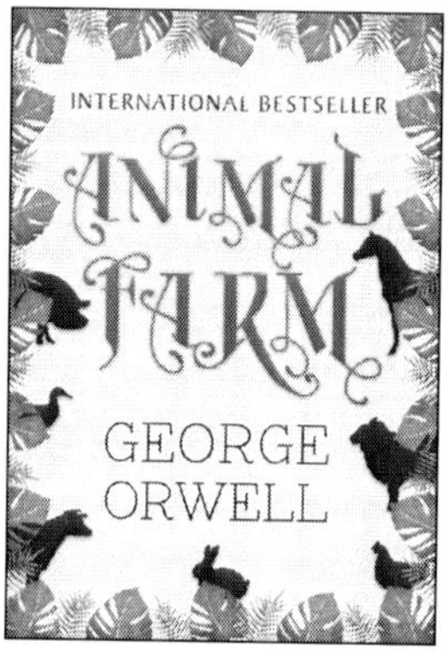

ANIMAL FARM

by George Orwell

Pages	:	128
Size	:	8.5x5.5 inches
Binding	:	Hardback
Language	:	English
Subject	:	Fiction/Classics
ISBN	:	9789387669062

Animal Farm is regarded in the literary field as one of the most famous satirical allegories of Soviet totalitarianism. Orwell based the book on events up to and during Joseph Stalin's regime. Orwell, a democratic socialist, and a member of the Independent Labour Party for many years, was a critic of Stalin, and was suspicious of Moscow-directed Stalinism after his experiences in the Spanish Civil War.

The plot is an allegory in which the pigs in a farm play the role of the Bolshevik revolutionaries and overthrow and oust the human owners of the farm, setting it up as a commune in which, at first, all animals are equal. The other characters have their parallels in the real world, but care should be taken with these comparisons as they do not always match history exactly and often simply represent generalised concepts.

The novel was chosen by TIME Magazine as one of the 100 best English-language novels from 1923 to the present.

OTHER HARDBACK BOOKS

- Abraham Lincoln by Lord Charnwood
  Biographies/Leaders, ISBN: 9789387669147
- Alice's Adventures in Wonderland by Lewis Carroll
  Children's/Classics, ISBN: 9789387669055
- Awakened Imagination by Neville Goddard
  Religion & Spirituality, ISBN: 9789389157185
- Be What You Wish by Neville Goddard
  Mind, Body & Spirit, ISBN: 9789388118163
- Becoming a Writer by Dorothea Brande
  Self Help/General, ISBN: 9789389157192
- Believe in Yourself by Joseph Murphy
  Mind, Body & Spirit, ISBN: 9789388118439
- Black Beauty by Anna Sewell
  Children's/Classics, ISBN: 9789388118262
- Civilization and Its Discontents by Sigmund Freud
  Social Sciences/General, ISBN: 9789388118279
- Feeling is the Secret by Neville Goddard
  Religion & Spirituality, ISBN: 9789389157208
- Gravity by George Gamow
  Sciences/Physics, ISBN: 9789388118705
- Great Speeches of Abraham Lincoln by Abraham Lincoln
  History/United States, ISBN: 9789387669154
- How to Attract Money by Joseph Murphy
  Self Help/Success, ISBN: 9789388118446
- How to be Filled with the Holy Spirit by A.W. Tozer
  Religion/Christianity, ISBN: 9789389157215
- How to Develop Self-Confi. and Pub. Speaking by Dale Carnegie
  Mind, Body & Spirit, ISBN: 9789388118286

Search the book by its ISBN

OTHER HARDBACK BOOKS

- How to Enjoy Your Life and Your Job by Dale Carnegie
  Self Help/General, ISBN: 9789388118293
- How to Stop Worrying and Start Living by Dale Carnegie
  Mind, Body & Spirit, ISBN: 9789387669161
- How to Win Friends and Influence People by Dale Carnegie
  Self Help/General, ISBN: 9789387669178
- Illust. Biography of William Shakespeare by Manju Gupta
  Biographies/Authors, ISBN: 9789387669246
- Madhubala by Manju Gupta
  Biographies/Cinems, ISBN: 9789387669253
- Meditations by Marcus Aurelius
  Non Fiction/Philosopy, ISBN: 9789388118781
- Mein Kampf by Adolf Hitler
  Autobiographies/Leaders, ISBN: 9789387669260
- My Experiments with Truth by Mahatma Gandhi
  Autobiographies/Leaders, ISBN: 9789387669277
- My Inventions: The Autobio. of Nikola Tesla by Nikola Tesla
  Autobiographies/Scientists, ISBN: 9789388118187
- Relativity by Albert Einstein
  Sciences/Physics, ISBN: 9789387669185
- Sense and Sensibility by Jane Austen
  Fiction/Classics, ISBN: 9789387669109
- The Alchemy of Happiness by Al-Ghazzali
  Religion & Spirituality, ISBN: 9789388118309
- The Art of Public Speaking by Dale Carnegie
  Self Help/General, ISBN: 9789388118477
- The Art of War by Sun Tzu
  Self Help/Success, ISBN: 9789387669321

Search the book by its ISBN

OTHER HARDBACK BOOKS

- The Autobiography of a Yogi by Paramahansa Yogananda
  Autobiographies/General, ISBN: 9789387669192
- The Diary of a Young Girl by Anne Frank
  Autobiographies/Memoirs, ISBN: 9789387669208
- The Dynamic Laws of Prosperity by Catherine Ponder
  Mind, Body & Spirit, ISBN: 9789388118194
- The Elements of Style by William Strunk
  Non Fiction/Skill, ISBN: 9789389157222
- The Game of Life and How to Play It by Florence Scovel Shinn
  Mind, Body & Spirit, ISBN: 9789388118316
- The Imitation of Christ by Thomas À Kempis
  Religion/Christianity, ISBN: 9789388118200
- The Knowledge of the Holy by A.W. Tozer
  Religion/Christianity, ISBN: 9789389157239
- The Magic of Believing by Claudie Bristol
  Religion/Christianity, ISBN: 9789388118217
- The Magic of Faith by Joseph Murphy
  Mind, Body & Spirit, ISBN: 9789388118712
- The Miracles of Your Mind by Joseph Murphy
  Mind, Body & Spirit, ISBN: 9789387669215
- The Origin of Species by Charles Darwin
  Sciences/Life Sciences, ISBN: 9789387669345
- The Path of Prosperity by James Allen
  Mind, Body & Spirit, ISBN: 9789388118323
- The Power of Awareness by Neville Goddard
  Mind, Body & Spirit, ISBN: 9789388118330
- The Power of Concentration by Theron Q. Dumont
  Self Help/General, ISBN: 9789388118224

Search the book by its ISBN

OTHER HARDBACK BOOKS

- The Power of Positive Thinking by Norman Vincent Peale
  Mind, Body & Spirit, ISBN: 9789388118729
- The Power of Your Subconscious Mind by Joseph Murphy
  Mind, Body & Spirit, ISBN: 9789387669222
- The Psychopathology of Everyday Life by Sigmund Freud
  Non Fiction/Psychology, ISBN: 9789388118231
- The Pursuit of God by A.W. Tozer
  Religion/Christianity, ISBN: 9789389157246
- The Quick and Easy Way to Effec. Speaking by Dale Carnegie
  Self Help/General, ISBN: 9789388118347
- The Richest Man in Babylon by George S. Clason
  Business & Economics, ISBN: 9789388118354
- The Science of Getting Rich by Wallace D. Wattles
  Self Help/Success, ISBN: 9789387669239
- The Seven Laws of Teaching by John Milton Gregory
  Self Help/General, ISBN: 9789388118460
- The Upanishads by Swami Paramananda
  Religion/Hinduism, ISBN: 9789388118774
- The World as I See It by Albert Einstein
  Non Fiction/Philosopy, ISBN: 9789388118248
- Think and Grow Rich by Napoleon Hill
  Self Help/Success, ISBN: 9789387669352
- Thought Vibration by William Walker Atkinson
  Non Fiction/Philosopy, ISBN: 9789389157253
- Wake Up and Live! by Dorothea Brande
  Mind, Body & Spirit, ISBN: 9789388118255
- Your Faith is Your Fortune by Neville Goddard
  Religion & Spirituality, ISBN: 9789389157260

Search the book by its ISBN